PUFFIN BOOKS
THE MAGIC DRUM

Sudha Murty was born in 1950 in Shiggaon in north Karnataka.
An M.Tech in Computer Science, she teaches the subject to
postgraduate students. She is also the chairperson of the Infosys
Foundation. A prolific writer in English and Kannada, she has written
nine novels, four technical books, three travelogues, one collection
of short stories and three collections of non-fiction pieces, including
*How I Taught My Grandmother to Read and Other Stories* (Puffin
2004). She is the recepient of the R.K. Narayan Award for Literature
and the Padma Shri 2006. Her books have been translated into all
the major Indian languages.

# THE MAGIC DRUM
## AND OTHER FAVOURITE STORIES

SUDHA MURTY

PUFFIN BOOKS

PUFFIN BOOKS

Published by the Penguin Group

Penguin Books India Pvt. Ltd, 7th Floor, Infinity Tower C, DLF Cyber City, Gurgaon 122 002, Haryana, India

Penguin Group (USA) Inc., 375 Hudson Street, New York, New York 10014, USA

Penguin Group (Canada), 90 Eglinton Avenue East, Suite 700, Toronto, Ontario, M4P 2Y3, Canada

Penguin Books Ltd, 80 Strand, London WC2R 0RL, England

Penguin Ireland, 25 St Stephen's Green, Dublin 2, Ireland (a division of Penguin Books Ltd)

Penguin Group (Australia), 707 Collins Street, Melbourne, Victoria 3008, Australia

Penguin Group (NZ), 67 Apollo Drive, Rosedale, Auckland 0632, New Zealand

Penguin Books (South Africa) (Pty) Ltd, Block D, Rosebank Office Park, 181 Jan Smuts Avenue, Parktown North, Johannesburg 2193, South Africa

Penguin Books Ltd, Registered Offices: 80 Strand, London WC2R 0RL, England

First published in Puffin by Penguin Books India 2006

Copyright © Sudha Murty 2006

All rights reserved

30  29  28  27  26  25

ISBN 9780143330066

For sale in the Indian Subcontinent only

Typeset in Sabon by Mantra Virtual Services, New Delhi
Printed at Replika Press Pvt. Ltd, India

A PENGUIN RANDOM HOUSE COMPANY

*This book is dedicated to all those great storytellers around the world who have passed on these stories from generation to generation.*

# CONTENTS

India has a rich tradition of storytelling. Texts like the Kathasaritasagara, Panchatantra and Jataka are a rich storehouse of tales which have been enjoyed by several generations of readers and listeners. These stories, full of humour and morals, are the ideal means to introduce the right values to young people.

If we look outside our country, we find all kinds of folktales that have been told to generations of children in every corner of the world. I have included a few such stories in this collection. Interestingly, while putting together these stories, I noticed that many Indian stories are about gods, curses and boons. They also often end with a marriage and the characters living happily after. Western stories, on the other hand, tend to emphasize logic and human intellect over other things, while middle-eastern ones have a lot of magic and supernatural elements.

I have tried to create a mix of these elements, though I have consciously left out stories which have gods and goddesses and supernatural beings solving problems, or even those in which animals are given human qualities. My stories do not have animals, gods, miracles or curses. My own favourites, and these are ones I loved hearing many years ago, are about how men and women, boys and girls, land themselves in trouble and how they extricate themselves from it. They are about human emotions and everyday human activities.

Though these tales have been gathered from all over the world, while retelling them I have set them all in India so that the Indian child can relate to them. The people have Indian names and they live in ancient Indian kingdoms.

I have rewritten many stories which I first heard as a child. Some others were told to me by people from other countries and some I have created myself.

I want to thank many people who have helped me to bring this book out, especially my publishers Penguin Books India.

Finally, I hope my readers, the children, will enjoy and remember them.

Bangalore                                         Sudha Murty
June 2006

## THE SUPERMEN

The men of Suvarnanagari were very lazy. They only liked to gossip and tell each other tall tales. As soon as the sun rose, the men would tuck into a hearty breakfast and start gathering in groups. Then they would spend the rest of the day telling each other impossible stories. They came back home only at lunch and dinner time.

Suvarnanagari had fertile land all around it, and if the men had spent even a little time in the fields, they would have reaped wonderful crops. But as they did nothing, all responsibilities ended up on the shoulders of the women, who had to slave the whole day. They cooked, cleaned, sent the children to school, worked in the fields, took the crops to the market—in short, they did everything. One day, the tired women got together and decided the men needed to be taught a lesson. Someone suggested writing to the king, who was known to be just and kind, about their problem. So a letter was written and sent off. The women went back to their work, but kept a sharp lookout to see if the king would send any help. But many days passed, and slowly the women began to lose hope. After all, why would the king of such a vast empire be concerned about the plight of a few women in a tiny village like theirs?

A month passed by and soon it was a full-moon night. The men ate their dinners and, because it was so beautiful and well-lit outside, they gathered again to chat and boast. That night, they were trying to prove to one another that they were capable of performing the most impossible tasks. As they sat talking, and the stories flew around, a tall and handsome stranger joined them. Seeing his noble features and intelligent eyes, each man wanted to prove himself better than the others and impress him.

One said, 'I knew the map of our kingdom even before I left my mother's womb. As soon as I was born, I ran to the capital and met the king. My mother had such trouble bringing me back home!'

Everyone was impressed with this story. But not to be outdone, a second man said, 'So what is so great about that? When I was just a day old, I could ride a horse. I sat on a big horse and rode all the way to the king's palace. He received me with a lot of love and we had the most delicious breakfast together.' At the thought of food, everyone got dreamy-eyed and the story was greeted with a round of applause.

Now a third man said, 'Huh! That's nothing. I sat on an elephant when I was a week old and had lunch with the king in his palace.'

Before the admiring murmurs could die down, a fourth one said, 'I was a month old when I flew like a bird and landed in the king's garden. He picked me up lovingly and even let me sit with him on his throne.'

While everyone seemed to be awed by these stories, the stranger spoke up. 'Do you four men know the king very well?'

'Of course we do!' they replied together. 'Our king knows and loves us. In fact, he is proud to have supernatural beings like us in his kingdom.'

The stranger looked thoughtful. 'That makes my task so much easier . . . You see, I work in the king's court. Some time back, the king had called four supermen to the city in order to repair a large hole in the city walls. As you know, we use the largest, toughest stones for building these walls, and they could be lifted and put in place only by these supermen. The four asked to be paid in gold bars and the king gave them the money. But that night itself they disappeared from the palace. I have been wandering the kingdom ever since, looking for them. The king has ordered me to find the four men and bring them back to the capital to finish the work. They will also have to return the gold they ran away with. It looks like my search has finally ended. I will take you four to the king, along with the gold you stole from him . . . And I shall be the rich one now.'

By the time the stranger finished telling this amazing story, the men's faces had turned ashen. What trouble had their lies landed them in? Together they dived at the stranger's feet.

'Save us!' they wailed. 'Those were all lies. We are just a bunch of lazy men. If you forget our stories, we promise to stop telling lies and do some honest work.'

The stranger smiled. 'So be it. I will tell the king there are no supermen in this village. Only hard-working, ordinary men and women.'

That night itself he left the village, and the women were sure they saw a happy twinkle in his eyes as he rode away on a handsome, white horse, fit to belong to the king's stables!

A FAIR DEAL

Himakar and Seetapati were two young men living in neighbouring villages. Once, a fair was being held nearby and they set off from their homes hoping to do some business there. Himakar filled his sack with some cheap cotton, overlaid it with a layer of fine wool and, slinging the sack over his shoulder, set off for the fair. Seetapati too collected wild leaves from some bushes, put a layer of fine betel leaves on top and made his way to the fair.

On the way, both stopped to rest under a big tree and got talking. 'I have the finest wool in these parts in my sack. They come from the most special sheep,' boasted Himakar.

'I have the best betel leaves in my sack. They are so soft they melt in your mouth. Usually I don't sell them, but this time I need the money, so I am going to the fair to sell them without telling anyone,' said Seetapati.

Quickly the two crooks struck a deal. They would exchange their goods and, since wool was more expensive, Seetapati would pay Himakar an extra rupee. But Seetapati had no money on him. So after agreeing to pay Himakar the rupee later, the two made their way home, secretly laughing at the other's folly.

However, it did not take long for them to discover that they had been duped.

The very next day, Himakar landed up at Seetapati's door and yelled, 'You cheat! Give me my rupee at least.'

Seetapati was drawing muddy water from his well and was unperturbed by Himakar's words. 'Of course I will pay,' he said. 'But first help me find the treasure lying at the bottom of this well. If we find it, we can divide it.' Both were soon hard at work and there was no more talk of wool or betel leaves. Himakar went inside the well where he would fill with muddy water the bucket Seetapati lowered to him. Seetapati would then pull it up. With each bucket Seetapati pulled up he exclaimed, 'Oh, no treasure here. Try again.'

This went on for a few hours. It started getting dark and Himakar realized that Seetapati was using him as free labour to clean his well. There was no treasure. He was sure that if he stayed much longer, Seetapati would abandon him in the well for good. So he gave a loud shout, 'Here is the treasure! Watch out, it is heavy.'

Seetapati was amazed that there really was treasure hidden in the well. He pulled hard, and as soon as he pulled up the bucket, he threw away the rope so that Himakar could not come up. But what, or rather, who did he find in the bucket but Himakar, covered in mud.

They started fighting again. 'You tried to cheat me!'

'You were going to leave me in the well!'

Soon it got too dark to argue and they left for their homes. But Himakar was not one to give up. He arrived at Seetapati's house after a few days, demanding his one rupee. Seetapati saw him coming and told his wife, 'I will pretend to be dead. You start crying loudly. Himakar will then have to give up trying to get the money from me.'

But Himakar was clever. As soon as he heard Seetapati's wife wailing, he understood the trick being played on him and rushed out to gather the villagers. 'My friend has died,' he shouted. 'Let's take his body for cremation.'

Seetapati's wife got scared. 'No, no, go away. I will arrange for the cremation myself,' she said.

But the villagers thought she was too grief-stricken to know what she was saying and carried Seetapati to the cremation ground. There Himakar told the villagers, 'It is getting dark. We cannot burn the body now. You go home and come in the morning. I will watch over him in the night.'

As soon as the villagers had gone, Himakar said to

Seetapati, 'Stop pretending now. Get up and give me my money . . .'

As they were fighting, a gang of thieves came to divide their loot in leisure at the cremation ground. They saw one person sitting on a pyre and another standing next to him. Both were arguing loudly. Thinking them to be ghosts, the thieves dropped their bag of stolen goods and fled at top speed. The two heard the commotion and saw the bag full of gold and silver ornaments lying on the ground. Quickly they divided it up between themselves. Himakar made sure he got an extra gold coin for the rupee that was due to him and the two men made their way back to their homes, the account settled at last!

## THE SEED OF TRUTH

Long ago, the country of Gandhara was ruled by the just and good king Vidyadhara. His subjects were very happy, but as the king grew older, everyone got more and more worried. The king did not have any children who could take over the reins of the kingdom after him.

The king was an avid gardener. He spent a lot of time tending his garden, planting the finest flowers, fruit trees and vegetables. One day, after he finished working in the garden, he proclaimed, 'I will distribute some seeds to all the children in the kingdom. The one who grows the biggest, healthiest plant within three months will become the prince or the princess.'

The next day there was a long line of anxious parents and children outside the palace. Everyone was eager to get a seed and grow the best plant.

Pingala, a poor farmer's son, was among these children. Like the king, he too was fond of gardening and grew beautiful plants in his backyard. He took the seed from the king and planted it in a pot with great care. Some weeks passed and he plied it with water and manure, but the plant did not appear. Pingala tried changing the soil and transferred the seed to another pot, but even by the end of three months, nothing appeared.

At last the day came when all the children had to go to the king to show the plant they had grown. They started walking to the palace, dressed in their best, holding beautiful plants in their hands. Only Pingala stood sadly, watching them go by. Pingala's father had watched his son working hard with the seed and felt sorry for him. 'Why don't you go to the king with the empty pot?' he suggested. 'At least he will know you tried your best.'

So Pingala too wore his best dress and joined the others outside the palace, holding his empty pot in his hand and ignoring the laughter around him. Soon the king arrived and began his inspection. The pots held flowers of different shades, beautiful and healthy, but the king did not look happy. At the end of the line stood Pingala, and when the king reached him, he stopped in surprise.

'Child, why have you come with an empty pot?

Could you not grow anything?'

Pingala looked down and said, 'Forgive me, Your Highness. I tried my best, I gave it the best soil and manure I had, but the plant would not grow.'

Now the king's face broke into a smile. He enveloped Pingala in his arms and announced, 'Here is the crown prince! I had given everyone roasted seeds, which would never grow, just to see which child was the most honest one and would admit he or she had not been able to grow anything. Only this boy told the truth. I am sure he will rule this kingdom one day with truth and honesty.'

And indeed that was what happened. When the king grew old and died, Pingala, who had learnt everything from him, came to the throne and ruled Gandhara justly for many years.

## HARIPANT THE WISE

During the reign of one of the Vijayanagar emperors, there lived a wise magistrate named Haripant. His verdicts were always fair and people came to him from all over the vast kingdom so he could settle their disputes.

In the city, there lived a greedy ghee merchant named Shiriyala Shetty. His shop always had twenty barrels of ghee, but of these, fifteen would be good and the remaining five adulterated. He would mix the adulterated ghee with the good one and sell it to the people. This went on for a long time, till finally the people got tired of being cheated and complained to Haripant.

Haripant got the ghee examined and found it to be adulterated indeed. He gave Shiriyala a choice of punishment. He could either drink the five barrels of adulterated ghee from his shop, or he could get hundred lashings, or pay a thousand gold coins to the treasury.

Shiriyala started thinking. Losing a thousand gold coins was too much and a hundred lashings too painful. So he decided to drink up the five barrels of ghee.

Though Shiriyala sold adulterated stuff in his shop, he had always made sure his own food was of the best quality. So after drinking one barrel of the bad ghee he started feeling sick. By the third barrel, he was vomiting. At this point he decided to opt for the lashings instead. But his was a pampered body, unused to any hard work. After ten lashes, he started trembling, by twenty he was giddy, and by forty he was half dead. 'Stop!' he screamed. 'I will pay the thousand gold coins! Just let me go.'

Finally Shiriyala had to pay the money, and he ended up suffering all three punishments, something he would not forget in a hurry. The people of the city got to use only the best quality ghee in their food from then on!

Another time, Gunakara, a poor coolie, was walking by Vibhandaka's clothes store. Vibhandaka was a rich merchant who owned a huge clothes store right in the centre of the town. It was a winter morning and Gunakara was carrying a large sack of waste from a nearby eatery to the rubbish dump. As he was passing by Vibhandaka's store, he slipped and fell. His sack opened up and the stinking waste lay all over

Vibhandaka's shop floor. The merchant immediately started screaming, 'Look at this mess. Clean it right away before my customers come.'

Trembling, Gunakara took a broom and bucket of water and started cleaning. He cleaned and polished till not a speck of dirt remained on the floor. But Vibhandaka would not give in so easily. 'The floor is wet,' he shouted. 'Get a cloth and wipe it.' Gunakara scratched his head. 'I don't have any cloth on me,' he said. 'Anyway, by the time your customers come the sun will be out and it will dry up. Or you give me a cloth and I will wipe the floor.' Now the merchant was even angrier. 'Is this a warehouse of old clothes? Where will I get a spare cloth from? You take off your coat and wipe the floor with it.'

This was too much. Gunakara was wearing an old, worn woollen coat, the only warm clothing he possessed.

'I am a poor man,' he tried to explain. 'Some rich person like you gave me this used coat for the winter. If I use this coat to clean the floor, what will I wear? Please let me go.'

But Vibhandaka was adamant. 'No. If the dirty smell persists after you go no customer will come to the shop. I will suffer big losses. My reputation will be ruined and I will become a pauper. So quick, take off your coat and clean up.'

By now, word of the argument had spread and a crowd had gathered. Haripant, on his way to court, heard the angry exchanges and pushed his way through the crowd. Everyone fell back. Justice would now be done, they were sure. When he had heard the entire story, Haripant turned to Gunakara. 'He is right. If you don't clean up well, Vibhandaka will suffer huge losses. Take off your coat and clean the floor.' A hush fell on the crowd. How could Haripant deliver such an unjust verdict? As the murmurs grew, Haripant held up his hand. 'I am not done yet,' he announced. 'There is a second part to my verdict.' Turning to the merchant he said, 'And you will compensate Gunakara's family for his untimely death.'

'What death?' howled an enraged Vibhandaka. Haripant was calm. 'Your complaint was based on an "if". "If" customers smelt the dirty smell, they would abandon your shop and you would be ruined. Similarly, "if" Gunakara loses his coat today, he may catch a cold and fever and die in a few days. His whole family depends on his earnings, so they may starve. Some of them might also die due to starvation. So you have to compensate his family.'

Haripant smiled as Vibhandaka stood looking worried. 'Gunakara, clean up,' he said. 'And, Vibhandaka, let him go inside the store and choose the best and warmest coat for the winter.'

The people who had gathered around applauded the clever verdict.

## THE LAST LADDOO

Once upon a time, there lived a miserly old couple, Devaiah and Devamma. They did not have any children and never spent a paisa on themselves. They never repaired their house or cooked good food. They wore old patched clothes and lived in a run-down little hut.

One day, a family moved into the village, close to Devaiah and Devamma's home. It was their little boy's birthday and they sent two delicious besan laddoos to the old couple. The two ate a laddoo each with great relish. For many days after that they could talk of nothing else. 'How soft they were! How the ghee dripped from them!' they exclaimed to each other. Finally, the old man, Devaiah, could take it no more. He told his wife, 'Let's buy the ingredients to make just two laddoos.' Devamma was delighted. Then she warned her husband, 'If I make the laddoos at home, the neighbours will get to know and want a share. Let's go to a secluded spot in the woods and cook there. That way no one will ever know.'

So the next day Devaiah got the ingredients from the market and they set off to the woods to make the laddoos. They indeed turned out delicious, but since they had never cooked anything like this before, and had not known the correct measurements, they ended up with three laddoos instead of two.

The old couple returned home with the bowl of sweets, dying to bite into them. But when they sat down to eat, a problem arose. How would they divide the three laddoos? 'It was my idea and I went to the market, so I must get two and you will get one,' said Devaiah. But Devamma was not one to give in so easily. 'I prepared the sweets. I must have two and you can have one.'

They started fighting. Day wore into night, but still they fought. At last Devaiah found a way out. 'Let us not talk to each other. Whoever breaks the silence first will get one laddoo and the other person two.' Devamma agreed and the two sat quietly, waiting for the other to talk first. Hours passed, but no one spoke. After some time they lay down, bored, with the bowl of sweets between them. Two days passed thus and the neighbours got suspicious. They came and banged on the door but the old couple would not answer in the fear of losing the bet. Then one neighbour climbed to the roof and, after removing a tile, peeped in. He saw the couple lying on the floor, a bowl between them. 'They are dead! The food is still lying there untouched,' he screamed.

Soon the door was broken open and the house was swarming with villagers. They discussed the funeral and wondered where the misers had hidden their wealth. Devaiah and Devamma heard everything but did not get up, in the fear of losing out on a laddoo. Finally the villagers carried them to the cremation ground and placed them on two pyres, though someone did suggest using only one for the two of them, as they were such misers. As the flames started licking their feet, Devamma jumped up, screaming, 'You win! You win! I don't want to die.'

Devaiah too jumped up happily. 'I have won! I will now eat two laddoos!' And the two rushed home, leaving a flock of bewildered, terrified villagers behind.

But alas, in the excitement of the funeral, the villagers had left the door of the hut open. The old man and woman rushed in to find a stray dog licking the last crumbs of the sweets from the bowl.

## THE TASTIEST OF ALL

King Shantivardhana ruled over the kingdom of Vaishali. He was a king who took his job very seriously. Every now and then he would leave the palace in the evening, dressed in the clothes of an ordinary man, to listen to what his people had to say about him and his ministers.

Once, he set out on a full-moon night. He walked into a little garden just in time to hear four girls debating an interesting issue: what is the tastiest thing of all? One said, 'Meat is the tastiest food of all.' Another said, 'No, it is liquor.' The third said, 'I think it is love, even though it is a feeling, not a food.' And the fourth said, 'It is hunger.'

The four friends argued amongst themselves, not knowing that the king was listening in the bushes behind them. The king had to go away after a while and he never got to hear the end of the argument. The next day, he woke up wondering who won the debate and what were the reasons the winner gave. He summoned the four girls to court. They came, trembling in fear, and were even more fearful when the king said that he had heard their conversation the night before. Now he said, 'Each one of you claimed a different thing as the tastiest of all. What were your reasons? If they are good, I will reward each of you.'

So the first girl said, 'I think meat is the tastiest thing in the world, even though I am a priest's daughter and have never tasted it.'

'Then how can you say so?' asked the king in surprise.

'Our house is opposite a butcher's shop. Every evening, the butcher throws the leftover bones and meat outside the shop. A big crowd of dogs gathers there and fights over these few pieces of meat. And after they are done, flocks of flies sit on the bones. So I think meat must be very tasty.'

The king liked her reasoning and gave her a reward. Then he turned to the second girl. 'Why did you say liquor is tasty? Have you ever had any?'

The girl shook her head. 'My father is a schoolteacher and no one in my family has had a drop of liquor ever. But I too stay opposite a shop—a liquor shop. There I see many people every day, spending so much money on their drinks. Often their families come and plead with them to come back home. Old parents and mothers with little children beg their sons, brothers and husbands to come home, but these people don't listen. They are only interested in their next glass. That is why I think liquor must be very tasty.'

The king liked her argument too and gave her a reward. Now the third girl said, 'I think love must be very tasty because I have seen how it transformed my sister. She used to be shy and obedient. But when she fell in love with a man my father did not like, she thought nothing of running away with him in the middle of a dark stormy night.' The king smiled and rewarded her too.

Then the last girl said, 'I agree with them. But there is one thing that is tastier than all this. It is hunger. If your stomach is full, the grandest of feasts will be tasteless, but on an empty stomach the most ordinary, even stale food will taste like nectar. Hunger makes our food tasty, whether we are young or old, rich or poor.'

The king now knew who was the winner of the argument. He gave the last girl a big reward for her clever words.

## THE CUNNING FRUIT

Udanka was a rich merchant with a vast business in north India. He had travelled all over the country and had seen many amazing sights during his travels. One day, his son Bhanuverma said to him, 'Father, you have seen so many new places. I have seen nothing. I am very keen to see the sea you described to me. Please let me go to the seaside.'

Udanka thought it was a good idea too and made arrangements for his son to travel to a south Indian town by the seashore, where he could stay with one of Udanka's friends. Thus Bhanuverma landed up in a town by the sea. His father's friend greeted him warmly and gave him a nice room in their house.

The next day, Bhanuverma set off to see the town. As he walked in the bazaar, he saw a man selling jackfruit. Now Bhanuverma had seen apples, oranges, mangoes, even jamuns, but jackfruit was something he had never set eyes upon. What a strange shape it had, and what a sweet smell! 'How do you eat this?' he asked the man selling it. 'Cut it, eat the fruit, and throw away the seed,' replied the man. When Bhanuverma heard that one big fruit cost only two annas, he was delighted and bought one. He carried it up to his room and proceeded to cut it open.

He ate and ate the sweet fruit. It was like honey. Finally when he was done, he realized that the gum from the fruit had made his hands all sticky. To get rid of the sticky gum, he wiped his hands on his dress, but that only made his dress sticky. He then tried washing his hands with water, but the gum remained. He slapped his head in despair and now his face too became sticky. Then he remembered there was a sack of cotton kept outside his door. He crept out quietly and tried to wipe his hands and face with the cotton. But he only managed to cover himself with cotton which now stuck fast on to his hands and face. The more cotton he used, the more it stuck to him.

Feeling ashamed, he went to the backyard, where he knew a pot of hot water was kept. By then it was evening and his host was calling him in for dinner. Not wanting to appear before him in that state, Bhanuverma hid behind a tree. The people of the house called out for him for some time, then thinking he must still be out somewhere, they took the vessel of hot water inside and shut the door. Bhanuverma looked this way and that. There was only the sheep-shed now for him to sleep in. He went there and lay down among the sheep.

That night, some thieves came to steal the sheep. When they saw Bhanuverma covered in cotton, they thought he was the biggest sheep of all and carried him away. Poor Bhanuverma dared not open his mouth to shout. At last, when they reached the outskirts of the town, they put him down. One close look at him and they fled, taking him to be a ghost.

Bhanuverma stood by the roadside, wondering what to do. A milkmaid who was walking by saw the young man covered in cotton and asked him what had happened. When he told her, she laughed for a long time. Then she said, 'You must always rub oil on your hands before you eat jackfruit. Otherwise the gum will stick to your hands and neither water nor cotton will take it off.'

She was very kind and took him to her house, where she gently removed all the cotton and the gum. Then Bhanuverma set off back to town.

After some weeks, when he came home, Udanka asked him, 'So what did you see? And what did you learn?'

Bhanuverma sighed and said, 'Father, I saw many strange sights, learnt many new things, but the biggest lesson I learnt was, whatever you do, never eat a jackfruit. It is the most cunning fruit of all!'

## NINE QUESTIONS FOR A PRINCESS

Princess Suryaprabha, who was very beautiful and intelligent, wanted to marry a man who was even more intelligent and learned than her. She was not too concerned about wealth or looks. So she said to her father, 'I have decided. Let any man ask me nine questions. If I am unable to answer even one of them, I will marry him.'

The king knew well how bright she was and was worried. 'And what if you answer all the questions?' he asked. 'Then he will be rejected and will not get a second chance.' The king had no choice but to agree to her condition and made the announcement in the kingdom. Many people arrived to try their luck. But the princess was too clever for them, and she answered each one's questions in no time. The king became more and more worried. He decided to talk to his most trusted friend, Ganapati Maharaj, who was a teacher, about this. Ganapati heard him out, then said he would send his brightest student Shashishekhar to question the princess.

The next day, a handsome young man appeared in court. He was dressed simply but his eyes shone bright with the light of knowledge. He announced that he had nine questions for the princess and, in no time, was sitting before her.

'How many stars are there in the sky?' was his first question.

Suryaprabha replied, 'There are as many stars as there are hair on a goat.'

'Which is the most beautiful child on earth?'

'For every mother, her child is the most beautiful.'

'What is the difference between truth and lies?'

'It is the difference between our eyes and ears. Our eyes will always see the truth but our ears can hear both truth and lies.'

'Which person has hands, yet is considered handless?'

'A rich man who does not share his wealth.'

'Who has eyes but is still blind?'

'A man without compassion, who does not see the suffering that exists in this world.'

Then Shashishekhar showed her a picture of a crumbling palace and asked what it meant. By now the princess was sure this was no ordinary man. But it did not take her long to give her answer.

'A house without a proper foundation, be it a palace, will collapse.'

He showed another picture—of an old lady collecting firewood, while carrying a heavy load on her back.

The princess smiled and replied, 'This picture depicts human greed. The woman has collected so much wood, yet she does not want to give up and go home.'

Now, the princess had answered seven questions accurately. There were only two left. Shashishekhar then asked a very clever question: 'Princess, which is the question you can't answer?'

Suryaprabha was stumped. If she told him, Shashishekhar would ask that question as the last one, and if she did not, she would lose anyway. She smiled and bowed her head. 'I accept defeat.'

Thus it came to be that the two wisest people in the kingdom got married and lived happily.

## 9

## Dead Man's Painting

Raghupati was a rich landlord who had a son called Sahadeva. The boy's mother died when he was very young, so Sahadeva was brought up by his father. He turned out a spoilt and mean child. When Sahadeva was about ten years old, his father married a second time. His new wife, Arundhati, was a sweet, good-natured woman.

Sahadeva was furious when his father got a new wife home and refused to behave well with his stepmother. After some time, when Arundhati gave birth to a boy, Sahadeva started hating her even more. He wanted nothing to do with his stepbrother. Raghupati tried his best to make him see reason, but he refused to listen. Then came a day when Raghupati fell very sick. Though he was treated by the best doctors in the kingdom, he soon realized his end was near. He decided to make a will and write down how his vast property should be divided after his death.

When he finished writing his will, he called his wife and told her, 'When you first read this, it may seem to you that I have done you a great injustice. But have faith. I only want to protect you and our son Janardan from Sahadeva's wrath.' Then he gave her a beautifully framed painting of his own face, done by one of the best artists of the kingdom, and told her, 'When our son Janardan is eighteen years old, take this to the king's minister, Krishnakant. He will see that justice is done to you.'

Arundhati was puzzled. 'Do you know Krishnakant?' she asked.

'No,' replied her husband. 'But I have heard a lot about his wisdom. He will know how to help you.'

A few days after this conversation, Raghupati died. Sahadeva could not wait for the rituals to be over so he could read the will. The day came when the will was finally opened and read out. In it Raghupati had left his large mansion and the surrounding fertile fields to Sahadeva. To Arundhati and Janardan he had left only a ramshackle outhouse and some dry scrubland surrounding it. Sahadeva was thrilled when he heard this. At least his father had seen sense on his deathbed! Happily he moved into the big house and poor Arundhati and her young son went to live in the broken-down little hut. But she remembered what her husband had told her and kept the painting safe with her, waiting for the day Janardan would turn eighteen.

Thus years passed, and on the day of Janardan's eighteenth birthday, Arundhati made her way to Krishnakant's house, the painting tucked under her arm. When she met him, she told him her entire story. Krishnakant was surprised. How was he to help her? After all, he had never seen, let alone known, Raghupati. But Arundhati was insistent. 'You must help,' she pleaded. 'My husband had great faith in your wisdom.' She left the painting with him and went back home.

After she had gone, Krishnakant laid the painting on the floor and looked at it carefully. He wondered what secret was hidden in it. Then he noticed the painting was crooked and pulled at a corner. To his surprise, the painting came out. And hidden behind it was a sheet of paper. A letter! 'Sir,' said the letter. 'You must be reading this many years after my death. In my life I heard many stories about you and how you helped people who were in trouble. I am sure my wife and son are in misery now. You have to help them somehow. The painting you are holding is my portrait. I can also tell you that the house where my wife now lives has ten golden bricks. It is up to you to extract those bricks and see she gets them without being harassed by my first son Sahadeva.' It was signed: Raghupati.

Krishnakant stood quietly for a while after reading

this, deep in thought. Then he smiled. He had a plan!

The next day, Krishnakant called Sahadeva and a few wise men to Arundhati's house. He got chairs laid out for everyone in the open field outside. To their surprise, he kept one chair separate and would not let anyone sit in it. When everyone was seated, he turned to the unoccupied chair and spoke to it. 'I will see that things are carried out according to your will. The wisest men of this village are my witness. You will at last go to heaven in peace.'

Then he turned around to the astonished group of people and said, 'I was visited yesterday by the ghost of Raghupati. Was he not a fair, tall man with a long nose and a mark on his forehead?' The people nodded in fear. Krishnakant had never met Raghupati when he was alive, so how did he know what he looked like? Surely, his ghost could not be around still?

Krishnakant now nodded and sighed sadly. 'So it was his ghost that came to me yesterday and said his wishes according to his will had not been carried out. And I promised to look into the matter.' He asked Sahadeva, 'Did your father leave you the big house and all the fields?' Sahadeva nodded. 'And he left the small outhouse and the land around it to your stepmother and stepbrother?' Sahadeva nodded again. 'And you are sure you have no claim to whatever there is in that house and on that land?' Sahadeva nodded again, vigorously.

Krishnakant now turned to Arundhati and said, 'Your husband's ghost wanted me to tell you that he wishes the house to be destroyed. Now that Sahadeva has said he has no interest in the house and whatever lies in it, I am ordering your house to be demolished right now.'

Arundhati, almost in tears, did not know what to say. She could only look on in horror as Krishnakant's men went up to her little hut with hammers and crowbars and started breaking it down. Sahadeva looked on happily till, imagine his dismay, the men came back to the group, holding ten golden bricks in their hands!

Krishnakant turned to Arundhati. 'Your husband left these bricks in the house. Since everything there belongs to you, and Sahadeva has said in front of everyone he has no claim on anything from there, you are now their rightful owner.' Taking a quick look at the empty chair he said, 'Raghupati is happy now. He will go to heaven at last, his soul in peace.'

With a twirl of his moustache, Krishnakant marched off, leaving behind an amazed Arundhati, now rich beyond her dreams, and a furious Sahadeva, who had been outwitted at last—all thanks to the painting of a dead man.

# THE WHITE CROW

Umasundari was a very talkative woman. She loved to sit and gossip the whole day. What the neighbours did, what they ate, what the village carpenter said to his mother-in-law—she enjoyed talking about all this. Her husband, Shivasundara, was a mild-mannered man and often told her to stop discussing other people's affairs. But she would never listen to him.

One day, Shivasundara was sitting outside his house, when he suddenly looked up and said, 'Umasundari! Look, what a beautiful crow is sitting on the white roof of our outhouse . . . but don't tell anyone about it.' Umasundari looked up and saw an ordinary black crow sitting on the roof. Why then had Shivasundara been so excited, and why had he asked her not to tell anyone about the crow?

Umasundari felt as though her stomach would burst with this news, so she went to her neighbour and said, 'Did you see our house today? Early in the morning a huge black crow was sitting on the white roof of our outhouse. I have never seen such a huge crow. My husband saw it too and he behaved like it was a big secret. He told me not to tell anyone. But I had to tell you. You will not tell anyone else, will you?' saying this much, Umasundari ran back home.

Her neighbour, whose name was Satyabhama, was having lunch. She got up midway and ran to her friend Vimalavati's house.

Vimalavati had finished her lunch and was cleaning her gold bangles. Satyabhama told her in a low voice, 'Have you heard the latest news? A massive crow was sitting on the roof of Umasundari's outhouse today. It was as big as an eagle and would not budge even though they tried to shoo it away. Maybe they have some hidden treasure and the crow knows about it . . . But don't tell anyone about this.' So saying she ran back home.

Vimalavati was very jealous. Her grandmother had told her long ago that unusual things always pointed to hidden treasure in a place. The presence of a huge crow must mean Umasundari had some treasure in her house. She was angry now. Here she was with a pair of worn-out old bangles, and Umasundari had discovered treasure! She ran to her husband Kamlesh.

Kamlesh was a writer and was trying to think of an idea for a story. Vimalavati told him, 'Stop writing imaginary stories. Look at Umasundari! They will soon have sacks of gold and diamonds without lifting a finger.'

Kamlesh too was upset to hear this. How could his neighbours get rich so quickly? He asked his wife how she had found out about the treasure. 'It seems there was a white crow sitting on the roof of Umasundari's outhouse. And that means there is a lot of treasure beneath it.'

Kamlesh had never liked Shivasundara; here was a good way to get back at him. He got up from his writing desk and went straight to the village headman. 'I have just got to know there is hidden treasure under Shivasundara's house,' he reported.

In their kingdom, the rule was that any treasure found below the earth belonged to the king, and not to the owner of the land. The headman rushed to Shivasundara's house with a few soldiers. 'We have to break down your outhouse,' they said. 'It is the king's order.'

Shivasundara tried to say something but no one listened. They started breaking down the house and digging away right then. After a lot of searching, they found nothing.

The angry headman now summoned Kamlesh and

asked, 'Who told you about the treasure?' Kamlesh pointed to his wife Vimalavati, who in turn pointed to Satyabhama, who pointed out Umasundari. She had to appear before the headman and confess she had exaggerated in the first place.

After that day, no one believed a word of what she said and nobody would sit down to chat with her. And Shivasundara would smile secretly to himself and say, 'I used Umasundari's loud mouth to break down the old outhouse. How much it would have cost me to do it myself! Now I will make a nice garden there, and the two of us will sit there and talk only to each other in peace!'

## 11

## THE HORSE IN THE BURROW

Niranjan was a very clever man. One day, as he was walking down the road, he met his friend Jayadev, who was returning from somewhere. He looked very sad, and in his hand he held the tail of a horse. 'What is the matter?' asked Niranjan.

'My horse died in an accident. By the time I heard about it and reached the place, a fox had taken away the body and only the tail was left.'

Jayadev was a poor farmer, and the horse had been his one expensive possession. Niranjan felt sorry for him. 'Give me the tail,' he told his friend. 'I will get a new horse for you.'

Jayadev had no idea how Niranjan would produce a new horse using only a tail, but he knew how clever Niranjan was, so he gave the tail to him and went back to his farm.

Niranjan walked down a forest path and saw a rabbit's burrow. He placed the tail at the mouth of the burrow and sat down next to it, holding on to the tail. Soon a rich merchant passed by, riding a beautiful horse. He looked in amazement at Niranjan sitting there holding the tail in his hands. 'What are you doing?' he asked.

'I was walking with my magic horse down this path when it ran into this burrow. You see, it can sense treasure and follow it anywhere. It has gone down the burrow to get the treasure and I am holding on to its tail. I will be rich when it comes up.'

The silly merchant believed this story. Then Niranjan said, 'I don't have a bag to keep the treasure. Can you give me one?'

Quickly the merchant replied, 'This bag has a hole in it. Why don't you go back to your village and get a bag? I will hold on to the tail till you come back. Here, take my horse, that will be quicker.'

Niranjan left riding the horse after pretending great reluctance. An hour passed by, but there was no sign of Niranjan, nor of the horse emerging from the burrow. The merchant pulled the tail and fell back! When he peeped into the hole, he saw of course there was nothing—no horse, no treasure, not even a rabbit!

Niranjan often used his wit to teach people a lesson. Once he met Dayananda, the milkman. Dayananda cheated his customers by adding water in their milk. That day he was carrying a large mud pot on his head, filled with milk. As soon as he saw Niranjan he said, 'You think you are so clever! But you won't be able to cheat me.'

Niranjan smiled and said, 'Dayananda, why should I cheat you? Particularly today, when there are so many clouds in the sky! It will rain any moment and I don't want to get drenched in the rain.'

'Oh, I have a long way to go! Is it going to rain?' Dayananda said, and forgetting the pot on his head, looked up. The pitcher fell and broke, and the milk spilt all over the road. That day Dayananda could not sell his milk-mixed-with-water to anyone!

## 12

## THE VERY EXPENSIVE COCONUT

Chandrakant was a miser. He hated spending money on anything and his wife was tired of his stingy ways. One day, Chandrakant went to a wedding. There he was served a coconut burfi. Chandrakant felt he had never tasted anything so good and decided he wanted another one.

He went back home and asked his wife to make him one. His wife looked at him and said, 'You hardly give me enough money to cook dal and rice. How will I make burfis? Go and buy a coconut at least and then I will make burfi for you.' So Chandrakant set off for the market. He saw a man sitting by the roadside with a heap of coconuts. He selected one and asked, 'How much is this for?' The man—who knew Chandrakant and his miserliness well, like everyone else in the bazaar—said, 'Five rupees.' Chandrakant nearly fainted when he heard this. Five rupees for a coconut! Seeing his face, the shopkeeper said, 'Walk ahead. You will come to a coconut grove ten kilometres from here. There you will get coconuts for three rupees.'

Chandrakant thought this was a wonderful idea. What if he had to walk ten kilometres, he would save two full rupees! So he walked, and after an hour reached the grove. When he saw the coconuts, he felt that even three rupees was a very high price for them and asked the gardener, 'Will you give it to me for one rupee?'

The gardener was busy. Without looking around he said, 'Ten kilometres from here, there is another coconut grove. There you can get it for one rupee.'

He would save two rupees more! Chandrakant set off at once. Tired, he reached the next coconut grove. But when he saw the coconuts, he felt like haggling again and asked the gardener, 'Will you give me a coconut for fifty paise?'

The gardener was upset. 'Walk ten kilometres further and you will reach the seashore where there are many coconut trees. Just pluck one, you will get it for free.'

Free! Chandrakant would walk to the end of the earth to get anything for free. He walked and walked and finally reached the seashore. Sure enough, there were rows of trees, with coconuts hanging from them. Anybody could just climb up and take one.

Chandrakant started climbing. Up and up he went. On the highest treetop he grabbed a delicious-looking coconut. Just then a gust of wind shook the tree and he lost his hold. He held on to the coconut for dear life. 'Help!' he shouted. A man came by on an elephant. When he saw Chandrakant hanging on to the coconut, he went up to the tree. Chandrakant begged him, 'Sir, will you stand on the elephant and hold my legs so that I can get down?'

The mahout said, 'I am in a hurry. But if you give me a hundred rupees, I will do it.'

A hundred rupees! But Chandrakant would break his bones if he remained there. He would have to pay up. He agreed sadly. The man stood on his elephant and grabbed his legs, but just then the elephant moved away and both of them were left hanging there.

Chandrakant was even more worried. Then, they saw a horseman and both of them begged, 'Will you stand on the horse and hold our feet so that we can get down?'

The horseman said, 'Only if you give me a thousand rupees.'

There was no other way out, so Chandrakant agreed.

But when the man grabbed their feet, the horse got scared and galloped away. Everyone fell in a heap and a bunch of coconuts fell on them. They broke bones, and Chandrakant had to pay a thousand rupees for their treatment. And all because he would not pay five rupees for a coconut!

# THE WISE KING

In the city of Manmathapura, which stood by the sea, there lived a young boy named Veeravara. He was brave and intelligent. He also longed for adventure, and when he became eighteen years of age, he took up a job on a ship so that he could travel and see other countries.

He travelled to many places on the ship and had many adventures. One day, when the ship was out at sea, a fierce storm began. The ship was tossed about and everyone was thrown overboard, including Veeravara. He managed to clutch on to a piece of wood and save his life. As he was floating in the sea, he lost consciousness. When at last he woke up, he found himself lying on the sandy shore of an unknown island, under the piercing rays of the sun.

Glad to be alive, he got up. He was on a large island,

and some miles inland, he could make out a city. Veeravara started walking in that direction. When he reached the city, to his surprise, he was greeted by a great crowd which was cheering him. Somebody came and garlanded him. He did not know what was happening. An elephant was brought forward and he was made to climb on to its back and sit on the howdah. A sad-looking old man was also sitting there silently. The elephant marched towards a palatial building. Veeravara asked the old man, 'Why did the people welcome a stranger like me in this grand fashion? What are they celebrating, and where are they taking me?'

The old man now looked sadder. 'This is an unusual island,' he explained. 'The people here are very intelligent but they have some funny rules. They are prosperous but they don't have a king. They feel if they choose a king from someone within themselves, he will be partial. So they wait for an unknown person to come to this island. When someone like you, a shipwrecked traveller, gets washed up at the shore, they make him their king. They are taking us to the palace. You are our new king now.'

'What happens to the previous king? And who are you?' Veeravara asked.

'I was the king till you came along. The old king is given a day to teach the new one the ropes. Then he is sent off to the next deserted island, where he has to look after himself. That's the rule.' Saying this, the old man pointed to an island. Veeravara could see it was covered with dense forest.

Now he knew why the old man was sad.

Veeravara was crowned king with great pomp. He quickly learnt his new job and became a good and fair king. But deep inside, a little part of him remained unhappy. When would the next shipwrecked person show up and he be sent off to the other island to live till the end of his days with wild animals and other retired kings?

As he thought about this, he came up with an idea. As long as he was the king, he had absolute power. He ordered his men to go to the island and to clear a part of the forest. There he ordered roads and houses to be built.

Soon there were roads, shops and pretty little houses on the island. People would go to the forest and see the wild animals; they gathered honey and fruits from the trees there, and in a few years, the island was no longer deserted but a cheerful little town.

Now Veeravara was not worried at all. When the next king appeared, he would not have to fend for himself in a forest. Instead, he would live in a little cottage and grow vegetables. Years passed and he got older. The people loved him and were sad whenever they thought he would no longer be their king. Then one day Veeravara called his people and said, 'It is good when you make a person from outside your king. He is fresh and unbiased. But this may not always be a good idea. What if the next person who comes here is a crook? You will make him king without knowing anything about him. Instead, let us have a system where the cleverest people of this island are chosen and rule the place together. Then no one person will have absolute power, and if anyone turns dishonest, you can always remove him from the council.'

The islanders liked the idea, and in a few days, chose their new rulers. Veeravara handed over charge of the kingdom to them and retired happily to his cottage, where he stayed till the end of his days.

## 14

# A Bottle of Dew

Ramanatha was the son of a rich landlord. His father left him large tracts of land when he died. But Ramanatha did not spend even one day looking after his land. This was because he had a funny idea, that there exists a magic potion which, if touched to any object, turns it into gold. He spent all his time trying to learn more about this potion. People cheated him often, promising to tell him about it, but he did not give up. His wife Madhumati was tired of this and also worried because she saw how much money Ramanatha was spending. She was sure that soon they would be left paupers.

One day, a famous sage called Mahipati came to their town. Ramanatha became his follower and asked him about the potion. To his surprise, the sage answered, 'Yes, in my travels in the Himalayas, I heard how you could make such a potion. But it is a difficult process.'

'Tell me!' insisted Ramanatha, not believing his luck.

'You have to plant a banana tree and water it regularly with your own hands. In winter, the morning dew will settle on its leaves. You have to collect the dew and store it in a bottle. When you have five litres of dew, bring it to me. I will chant a secret mantra, which will turn it into the magic potion. A drop of this potion will transform any object into gold.'

Ramanatha was worried. 'But winter is only for a few months. It will take me years to collect five litres of dew.'

'You can plant as many trees as you want. But remember, you must look after them yourself and collect the dew with your own hands.'

Ramanatha went home and, after talking to his wife, started clearing his large fields which had been laying empty all these years. There he planted rows and rows of banana trees. He tended them carefully and during the winter months collected the dew that formed on them with great care. His wife helped him too. Madhumati gathered the banana crop, took it to the market and got a good price for it. Over the years, Ramanatha planted more and more trees and they had a huge banana plantation. At the end of six years, he finally had his five litres of dew.

Carefully, he took the bottle to the sage. The sage smiled and muttered a mantra over the water. Then he returned the bottle and said, 'Try it out.' Ramanatha sprinkled a few drops on a copper vessel and waited for it to turn to gold. To his dismay, nothing happened!

'This is cheating,' he told the sage. 'I have wasted six precious years of my life.'

But Sage Mahipati only smiled and called Madhumati to come forward. She came with a big box. When she opened it, inside glinted stacks of gold coins!

Now the sage turned to the astonished Ramanatha and said, 'There is no magic potion that can turn things into gold. You worked hard on your land and created this plantation. While you looked after the trees, your wife sold the fruits in the market. That's how you got this money. It was your hard work that created this wealth, not magic. If I had told you about this earlier, you would not have listened to me, so I played trick on you.'

Ramanatha understood the wisdom behind these words and worked even harder on his plantation from that day on.

## 15

## TWO THIEVES

Saranga was a clever minister in the court of King Devaprasanna. Saranga was such a good adviser that none of the neighbouring kings could ever succeed in attacking the kingdom. Naturally, they were very jealous of Devaprasanna and his brilliant minister.

Saranga was also a great patron of the arts. Many artists, writers and thinkers gathered in his house. He gave them shelter and the means to work on their art. One day, two strangers appeared at his doorstep. 'We have been wandering in many places. We heard you are kind to talented people, so we have come to ask you for shelter,' they said.

'What are your talents?' asked Saranga.

'I can bark like a dog,' said one. 'My imitation is so good that even real dogs get confused. And my friend here can crow better than a cock.'

'What have you been doing all this while with these talents?' asked Saranga, amazed.

Now the two friends looked embarrassed. Finally they said, 'We will be honest. We were thieves and used these talents to confuse the owners of the houses we robbed. Now we have decided to mend our ways and do some honest work. That is why we have come to you.'

Saranga decided to let the two stay in his house, even though his other guests protested. He felt they were truly repentant and should be given a chance. So the two stayed with him and became a part of his group.

Now, Himabindu was a wicked old king of a neighbouring kingdom. Several times he had wanted to invade Devaprasanna's kingdom but had failed miserably because Saranga would always foil his plans. He wanted Saranga to become his minister, then he could easily conquer Devaprasanna's kingdom.

One day, he sent a letter to Devaprasanna: 'I want to honour your minister Saranga. I want him to come to my kingdom and give my ministers some lessons in statecraft. Please send Saranga to my kingdom and allow him to stay here for a few days.'

Saranga was suspicious when the king informed him about the letter. But Devaprasanna wanted to be on good terms with his neighbours, so he said, 'Why don't you go? If you suspect something is wrong, just come back.'

Saranga now had no choice but to go to Himabindu's court. He took his group of artists and writers with him, as well as the two ex-thieves.

Himabindu welcomed Saranga with great respect. Saranga too had come with many gifts for the king, among them a beautiful, rare shawl. Finally, the king sat down to talk to him. 'Saranga, I know you are the brain behind Devaprasanna's success as a king. You have served him for many years. Why don't you work for me now? I will make you richer than ever. You will be my chief minister.'

Saranga, who had suspected all along that something like this would happen, had his answer ready. 'My family has served King Devaprasanna for many generations. I cannot leave his service. I am sorry.' As soon as the words had left his mouth, Himabindu flew into a rage and ordered that Saranga be thrown into prison.

When his friends, who were waiting in another room, heard about this, they were shocked. How could they save their beloved Saranga now? They came up with many plans, none of which could be carried out by a bunch of artists. Finally, one said, 'Queen Sanmohini is the king's favourite queen. She is beautiful and intelligent. She loves rare art objects, especially shawls.'

'But we came with only one shawl, and Saranga presented it to the king. If only we could get it back . . .'

The two former thieves listened to the discussion in silence. After some time, they walked out quietly. They went to the royal chamber where the gifts were piled up. A ferocious-looking guard stood at the door and frowned at them. Quickly, they slipped behind a tree, and one of them began barking like a dog. The guard was startled. How could a dog enter the royal palace? Surely, if the king heard the noise it was making, the guard would be out of a job!

He rushed off to find the dog while the other friend went inside and found the shawl. Then they quickly made their way back to the group of friends, who were still deep in discussion. 'Here is the shawl,' they said, giving it to the oldest and wisest person in the group. 'Now you can present it to the queen.'

The man took the shawl to the queen. She was delighted with the shawl. 'What a beautiful design! Such soft wool! How much do you want for this?'

Saranga's friend bowed low and said, 'Your Highness, I don't want any money for this. But please request the king to free our dear friend Saranga.'

The queen agreed. That night, when Himabindu came to have dinner with his favourite queen, she served him the most delicious dishes. He was delighted, and after tucking into a huge dinner, leaned back happily and asked, 'What is it, my dear? You look worried. Is there anything you desire?'

Quickly the queen said, 'I have heard that a clever

minister called Saranga has been imprisoned by you. He is said to be a wise man. Should we treat him like this? Why don't you free him? Just for me . . .'

The king, already sleepy after his enormous dinner, said, 'Yes, yes,' and ordered Saranga's release.

Saranga was greeted by his friends with great delight. Then someone said, 'We should leave the kingdom before the king discovers we stole his shawl and gave it to the queen.'

Everyone agreed and, quietly, the group packed their bags and left the palace. But there was a problem when they reached the city walls. The huge gates were locked! The soldier guarding them said, 'That is the law. I cannot open them till it is dawn.'

Saranga and his friends sat down to wait. As the hours passed, they grew more and more nervous. What if the king got to know about the theft before they could escape? Finally, one of the two former thieves got up. He climbed a tree near the soldiers guarding the gates and crowed loudly like a cock. The soldiers jumped up and, thinking it was morning already, rushed to open the gates. Saranga and his group were ready. They left as quickly as they could and reached their own kingdom by early morning.

In the meantime, King Himabindu woke up after a long refreshing sleep and saw his queen dressed in a beautiful sari with an even more exquisite shawl around her shoulders. But why did the shawl look familiar?

When he quizzed her, she told him the story of the man who gave it to her as a present and asked for Saranga's release in return.

The king now ordered his men to bring him the shawl presented by Saranga, but it was nowhere to be found! Finally he understood what had happened. He could only smile at the cleverness of Saranga and his friends. It was better to have such clever people as friends than enemies, he decided, and from that day the two kingdoms became friendly neighbours.

## 16

## THE BEST FRIEND

Keshava was a lonely washerman. His only friend was his donkey. They worked together the whole day, and often Keshava would talk to the donkey and pour out his heart to it.

One day, Keshava had many clothes to wash. He was walking home with the donkey when suddenly he felt very tired. He tied the donkey to a tree and sat down to rest for a while. Nearby, there was a school. The window of a classroom was open, and through it, the noise the children were making could be heard. Then came the voice of the teacher. He was scolding the students. 'Here I am, trying to turn you donkeys into human beings, but you just won't study.'

As soon as Keshava heard these words, his ears pricked up. What! Here was a man who could actually turn donkeys into humans! This was the answer to his prayers. Impatiently, he waited for school to be over for the day. Then, when all the children had gone home, and only the teacher remained behind to check some papers, Keshava entered the classroom.

'What do you want, Keshava?' asked the teacher, who knew him well.

Keshava scratched his head and said, 'I heard what you said to the children. Please take my donkey and make him into a human being. I am very lonely, and this donkey is my only friend. If it became a human, we could have such good times together.'

The teacher realized Keshava was a simpleton and decided to fool him. He pretended to think for a while, then he said, 'It will take some time. Give me six months. Oh yes, and it is an expensive request. It will cost you a thousand rupees.' The foolish washerman agreed and rushed home to get the money. He left the donkey with the teacher and settled down to wait.

Exactly six months later, Keshava appeared at the teacher's door. Now, the teacher had been using the donkey for his own work and had found it most useful. Not wanting to give it up, he said, 'Oh, your donkey became so clever that it ran away.'

'Where is he now?' asked Keshava.

'He is the headman of the next village,' said the cunning teacher and slammed his door shut.

Keshava trotted off to the next village. There the

village elders were sitting under a tree, discussing some serious problems. How surprised they were when Keshava marched up to the headman, huffing and puffing, grabbed his hand and said, 'How dare you? You think you are so clever that you can run away? I spent a thousand rupees to make you a human from a donkey. Come home at once!'

The headman understood someone had played a trick on Keshava. 'I am not your donkey!' he said. 'Go to the sage sitting in the forest. He will explain everything to you.'

Sadly, Keshava went to find the sage. He found him sitting under a tree, deep in meditation. He crept up and quickly grabbed the sage's beard. 'Come back now!' he shouted. 'Enough of this!'

The startled sage stood up and somehow calmed Keshava. When he finally heard what had happened, he had a good laugh. Then he told the washerman, 'The teacher made a fool of you. Your donkey must be still with him. Go and take it back from him. And then try to make some real friends, who will talk with you and share your troubles with you. A donkey will never be able to do that!'

## 17

## Good Luck, Gopal

Gopal was a good-natured but very dull boy. His father was a learned man and despaired for his son. 'You must study hard, Gopal,' he would tell his son. 'Without learning, you will remain a frog in the well.'

Poor Gopal tried very hard, but he was rather stupid and could not progress much with his studies. Some years later, his father died. By then Gopal was married and had a family to look after. But no one would give him a job, he was so silly. One day, there was no food in the house and Gopal's wife said to him, 'I have heard that our king is very fond of good literature. Why don't you write him a nice poem? Perhaps he will like it and give you a reward.'

Gopal had no choice but to agree, and he set off to

have a bath in the pond before sitting down to write his verse. At the pond he saw a pig, covered in mud, rubbing its back against a tree trunk. The pig was rubbing so hard that Gopal was afraid its skin would come off. So he said, 'Don't rub so hard. It is not good for you. It will put your life in danger.' Then, unable to think of anything else to write, he put down these words on a palm leaf and made his way to the palace.

By the time he reached there, it was evening and the palace gates were shut. The guard refused to let him in. 'Please,' Gopal pleaded. 'I have an important document for the king.' One of the guards took pity on him and agreed to leave the palm leaf where the king would see it in the morning.

Gopal handed over the palm leaf and went to rest in a dormitory. The royal guard placed the palm leaf on the king's table for him to see when he woke up.

The next morning, the royal barber came to trim the king's hair and was sharpening his knife against a stone, while the king waited for his haircut. Just then, the king's eyes fell on the palm leaf and he read aloud what was written on it: 'Don't rub so hard. It is not good for you. It will put your life in danger.'

The barber had been sharpening his knife because he planned to use it to kill the king. An evil minister had made him agree to take on the job. When he heard the king's words, he was scared out of his wits. The king knew his plan! He fell at the king's feet and begged for forgiveness. He also told the king about the minister and how he had made the barber agree to carry out the killing.

The king got the minister arrested and threw him into prison. Then he realized the words on the palm leaf had saved his life and he wanted to know who had written them. An astonished Gopal was dragged out of bed and presented before the king, who showered him with rewards and appointed him as the court astrologer.

A few days later, the queen could not find her favourite necklace. The whole palace was in a turmoil. Even the king was worried. If the queen did not get the necklace soon, he would have to face the consequences. So he summoned Gopal. 'You saved my life with your divine powers. Now help us find this necklace,' he commanded.

Poor Gopal, he did not know what to do. Trembling, he said, 'I can look at the past and predict the future only when I am alone. Please let me go to my room. I will come to you shortly with the whereabouts of the necklace.' Then he rushed to his room, bolted the door and lamented to himself loudly, cursing his wife for the situation, 'O lady, your desires have doomed your husband. Because of you your husband is in trouble, and you may be a widow soon. Your husband escaped once, but this time there is no escape for him.' On the other side of the door, a maidservant heard these words and started trembling. She had stolen an earring once with the help of her husband, who was the palace gardener, and this time, the two had got greedy and stolen the queen's precious necklace. Hearing Gopal's words, she thought he was talking to her and knocked on his door. As soon as he opened it, she fell at his feet and begged forgiveness. Then she told him where the necklace and the earring were kept. Gopal happily went and told this to the king and once again everyone marvelled at Gopal's divine powers.

A few weeks went by peacefully. Then one day, a messenger arrived from the neighbouring king. In his hand he held a wooden box, its lid shut tight. The message from the king said: 'We have heard much about the new astrologer in your court and his powers. Here is a test. Can he tell what is in this box?'

The court now turned towards Gopal. The kingdom's reputation was hanging on his words. Gopal, who of course had no idea what was in the box, muttered his father's words to himself, 'Oh frog, your life is indeed becoming very difficult.'

No one understood what he meant, but the messenger looked amazed. He opened the lid and out hopped a frog!

By now the king was very impressed with Gopal and showered him with gold coins. But Gopal had had enough. 'I was told I would be able to predict only three things correctly,' he told the king. 'I have finished making all three prophecies. Now please let me return to my wife.' Sadly, the king agreed and sent Gopal home, but not before plying him with many more gifts. Gopal and his wife lived the rest of their lives in happiness and comfort.

## 18

## NAKUL'S FIRST LESSON

Bhaskar was a wealthy, worldly-wise merchant. He had one son, Nakul. One day, Bhaskar fell ill and realized he was going to die. So he called Nakul to him and gave him some advice. 'When you do business and travel to foreign lands, make sure you know the local culture well. Try to gain as much information as you can before you go there, as only your knowledge and presence of mind will come to your help in an unknown land.'

Nakul listened to his father's words carefully. Bhaskar died soon after and Nakul began to look after the business. Once, he had to sail to a faraway country on work. There, he stayed in an inn. He got talking to its owner and, without realizing, ended up telling the man all about his life, the business and his father.

Next day, he went to the market, and was amazed when a one-armed man rushed up to him and said, 'Your father took one of my arms as a loan. You must return it to me.' Not knowing what to do, Nakul asked for a day to think about this. Then, a woman came up to him and said, 'Your father married me. He used to send me money every month. Now that he is dead, you must give me money.' Again Nakul asked for a day's respite and walked on. He stopped at another inn and ate some breakfast. When he went to make his payment, the owner said, 'I only want you to make me happy.' Though he had to pay only two coins, Nakul gave the man five, but still he said he was unhappy. Puzzled, Nakul walked on.

A man invited him to a game of dice. Poor Nakul did not know that they were playing with a trick dice. He lost all the games. But the man who won set an unusual condition. 'You must drink all the water in the sea, or else give me all the goods in your ship.' Poor Nakul again said he would be back the next day with his answer.

That night, as he lay in his bed, he remembered his father's words, 'In a foreign land only your wits will come to your aid.'

The next morning, as soon as he went to the market, the one-armed man appeared before him. Nakul greeted him with a big smile and said, 'You were right. My father took many hands like yours and our house is full of hands. Give me your other hand. I will find the matching one and send it to you.' The man ran away in fright.

Then he found the woman who claimed to have been married to his father. 'Mother!' he shouted. 'My father was wrong not to have told us about you. Now you are like a second mother to me. Come home with me and help my mother in the fields.' The woman too made a quick getaway when she heard this.

Next he went to the hotel. The owner was standing outside. Nakul shouted to him, 'Hail the king! Your king is the best in the world!' The man had no choice but to answer, 'You are right. I am happy you think so.'

'If you are happy, I have paid for my meal,' said Nakul and went to find the man with the dice. When he found him, he said, 'I have thought over the challenge. I will drink all the water in the sea. But you have to bring me the water in jugs.' That man too ran away when he heard this.

Nakul went on to do a lot of business in that country and returned home richer—in wisdom too!

## 19

## GOLDEN SILENCE

Somesh was a boy of ten. He was a chatterbox and loved to talk with anyone who had the time to listen to him. Sometimes he would talk so much that his parents would have to tell him to stop and rest his tongue awhile!

Every night, he would lie down to sleep with his father, who would tell him a story. At that time Somesh was all ears. He would listen to his father's story attentively and then drift off to sleep. One day, he listened to his father's story as usual. The next morning when he woke up, his parents were shocked. There was pin-drop silence in the house. Somesh had stopped talking! At first they were relieved, thinking he was playing a game. But when he did not talk even after many days, they got worried. They took him to the best medicine men in the country, to all the sages and holy men they could find, but no one found anything wrong with him. Neither did any of their treatments have any effect on the boy.

Years passed and Somesh grew into a young man. His parents and everyone who knew him now thought him to be dumb. One day, he was travelling with his father's friend Lokesh to another village. They sat down to rest under a huge banyan tree. A crow was cawing loudly on one of the branches. Lokesh was telling Somesh a very funny story involving a milkman, his cow and the village goonda and was mighty irritated to have the crow cawing loudly overhead as he spoke. Finally he could take it no longer. The crow was spoiling a perfect story! He first tried to shoo it away, but it paid him no heed. Then he picked up a stone and threw it at the crow, thinking that would make it fly away. Instead, the stone hit the crow and it fell dead.

Lokesh was horrified. He had not meant to kill the bird at all. As he stood staring at the dead form lying under the tree, he did not realize when Somesh had come up behind him. He was stunned when he heard a voice behind him say, 'Foolish crow, if only you had kept your mouth shut and been silent, you would not have met this end.'

Lokesh forgot all about the crow and turned to stare at Somesh. The boy had spoken! 'Say it again, Somesh!' he begged. But Somesh just smiled mysteriously and refused to utter one more word. Lokesh hurried back to the village and told Somesh's father the story. Now Somesh's parents begged him again and again, 'Speak once more, son. For the sake of your dear old parents.' But it seemed as if Somesh did not know how to talk, and everyone put the incident down to Lokesh's imagination.

After that day, Somesh's father and Lokesh, who had been business partners and friends for many years, stopped speaking to each other. They took on other partners in business and suffered losses. They were miserable as they had no one to share their deepest sorrows and joys with. Somesh saw all this, and one day, as he sat down to eat with his father, he noticed his father was just toying with his food. His mind was clearly elsewhere. Suddenly Somesh spoke again, 'If Lokesh Uncle had remained silent, he would have been your friend still. You were right, Father, silence is golden and speech is silver.'

His father nearly fainted when he heard this. Suddenly he remembered the bedtime story he had told his ten-year-old son. It was about a king who lost his kingdom because he was too busy talking to prepare for war. And his final words before his son had drifted off to sleep were: Silence is golden, speech is silver.

He hugged his son and explained, 'That was just a saying. How I have longed to hear you talk again. Please do not do this again. I will never complain about your chattering again.'

From that day on, Somesh spoke again, but he remembered to think carefully before he opened his mouth!

## 20

## EMPEROR OF ALAKAVATI

Sumant was a bright young man who lived in Vidishanagara in ancient India. He had been orphaned when he was very young and had had to fend for himself from a young age. As a result, he was smart and cunning.

One day, he felt very hungry. He went to a sweet-shop just in time to hear the shopkeeper tell his son, 'Child, I am very sleepy. Look after the shop while I take a nap. Call me only if something important comes up.' Sumant immediately smelt an opportunity. He hung around outside the shop for some time. Then he went in and announced loudly, 'I am your father's best friend's son. Give me the best sweets in the shop.' The boy, who had never seen Sumant earlier, was suspicious. 'What is your name?' he asked. 'My name is Fly,' said

Sumant, helping himself to some delicious jalebis. As he sat eating, the boy ran to his father. 'Father! Fly is eating the sweets. What should I do?'

The sweet-shop owner was in deep sleep. He mumbled, 'How much can a fly eat? Let him be. Now go away.' So saying, he turned over and started snoring loudly. Sumant, meanwhile, had finished the jalebis and had pulled a pile of gulab jamuns towards him. The poor boy could do nothing but watch him demolish them all. Finally Sumant took two boxes of the best sweets in the shop and left without paying a single paisa.

He walked straight to Kanaka Chandra's shop. Kanaka Chandra was the biggest miser of Vidishanagara. Sumant presented the boxes to him and said, 'Here is a present for one of Vidishanagara's greatest men. I am only a poor man. I have nothing more to give you.'

Kanaka Chandra peeped into the boxes and was delighted to see them chock-full of delicious mouth-watering sweets. 'Sir,' said Sumant humbly, 'I have only one request. Can I have these two boxes back, please?' Kanaka was only interested in the sweets, so he said graciously, 'Of course, of course. Please go inside the house and tell my wife to give you two vessels to put these sweets in. Then you can take the empty boxes.'

Sumant walked into the kitchen, where the wife was cooking lunch. 'Your husband has asked you to give me two gold coins,' he announced to the astonished woman. 'What! Are you out of your mind? My husband would never say such a thing!' said the woman. So Sumant called out at the top of his voice, 'Your wife is refusing to give me what you had asked for.'

Kanaka was in the middle of negotiating a handsome deal with a merchant. Irritated by this disturbance, he called out to his wife, 'Just give him what he wants.' So Sumant walked out, whistling loudly, with the two coins in his pocket. Of course he had left the boxes and the sweets for Kanaka and his wife.

Now he walked to the outskirts of the city and buried one coin under a bush. Then he sat down next to it, a stick in hand.

As soon as he heard the sound of a horse approaching, he started waving his stick around and pretending to examine the nearby bushes. The soldier sitting on the horse watched Sumant behaving in this odd fashion. When he could no longer hold back his curiosity he asked, 'What are you doing?' Sumant, pretending to be very busy, answered, 'My magic cane leads me every day to a hidden treasure buried under a shrub. Today it led me here and I am looking for the treasure.' Saying this, he started digging under the shrub where he had just hidden the coin and pretended to find it with a triumphant yell. The soldier could not believe his eyes and got down from his horse. He examined the coin closely. Then he said, 'Give me your magic stick. You can take my horse in return. It's the best you can get in this kingdom. And that is a fair deal.' Sumant pretended to hesitate. 'No, no. This stick is my life. I cannot part with it.' After much cajoling and threatening, the soldier managed to take the stick from Sumant, who in turn rode off with the magnificent horse.

He rode all day, till he reached a rich farmer's farm. He knocked on the door and said, 'I am a weary traveller. Can you give me and my horse shelter for the night?' The farmer saw the beautiful horse and agreed to shelter them for the night. The horse was given a place in the stables and Sumant a room to sleep in.

The next morning, Sumant woke up early and asked the farmer, 'Can you give me a sieve?' The farmer, though astonished at this strange request, gave him one. Then he told his servant to follow Sumant. Sumant first went to the stable, where he collected some fresh dung from his horse, then he went to his room, and pretending great secrecy, started sieving the dung. He knew all the time that the servant was watching him, and making sure the man could see what he was doing, Sumant produced the other gold coin from the dung.

The servant excitedly reported everything to his master. The farmer immediately made his way to Sumant, who was grooming his horse, as if readying to leave.

'Tell me about this horse,' he demanded. 'Tell me only the truth, mind you.' Sumant, pretending to be scared, stammered, 'T-this h-horse has m-magical powers. Once a d-day it produces a g-gold c-coin in its d-dung.' The farmer, who was very greedy, said, 'Give me the horse. I will give you a hundred gold coins in return.' Sumant pretended to hesitate for a while and then, making a show of great reluctance, handed over the reins of the horse to the farmer and trotted off on foot, a bag full of coins jingling in his pocket.

It was evening by the time he reached the next village, and he took shelter in the house of an old couple. When he went out into the nearby forest in the morning, he spotted an old woman sitting outside a small hut. Her young granddaughter was washing some clothes nearby. He told the old woman, 'Do as I say, and you'll be rich.' So saying, he went back to the couple with a bottle full of a green liquid in his hand. 'What is this?' asked the old man, when he saw Sumant. 'It is a medicine to make you young. I discovered it during my wanderings in the Himalayas,' answered Sumant. The man asked, 'Do you have any proof of its effects?'

'I'll show the effects to you only if you pay me in gold,' said the wily Sumant, and having struck the deal, led them to the old woman's hut in the forest.

The old woman was sweeping her courtyard. Sumant pointed her out to the couple and said, 'I'll give her my medicine. Just wait and see what happens.' Then he marched up to her and, slipping some money into her hand along with the medicine, said, 'Drink this.'

The woman had the medicine and disappeared into the house. Immediately her granddaughter emerged wearing identical clothes and started sweeping the courtyard, as if nothing had happened.

The couple was impressed. 'Give us the medicine,' they clamoured. Sumant took a hundred coins from the man and gave him some herbs to make him unconscious. Then he told the wife, 'He is sleeping. He is so old, it will be some time before the medicine takes effect. He will be a young man when he wakes up. I will give you your dose tomorrow.' But the old woman would not agree. 'Give me my dose now. If my husband wakes up and sees his wife is an old woman, he will start looking for someone younger.' Sumant, pretending to be very reluctant, gave her a spoonful of the herbs which made her unconscious—only after she had paid him another hundred coins, of course.

Thus many days passed and Sumant made a living by cheating ordinary folk with his smooth talk and tall promises.

The king of Vidishanagara heard about him and ordered his arrest. Sumant walked into the king's trap one day and was produced before him. 'You are a cheat,' said the king. He ordered his soldiers. 'Put him in a bag and when the sun sets, throw him down the mountain cliff.' The soldiers stuffed Sumant into a bag and left him under a tree, waiting for the sun to set. Inside the bag, Sumant's clever brain was ticking away.

Suddenly he heard what sounded like the footsteps of an elephant nearby. He started shouting, 'Help! I don't want to be king. Help, someone, please!'

The man riding the elephant heard these strange words coming out of the bag and opened it. Sumant jumped out and said, 'Thank you, sir. Our king has no heir. But this morning, his elephant touched me with its trunk and he decided I should be the king after him. When I said I was just an ordinary man, he tied me in this sack and left me here till I agreed.'

The stranger was tempted. 'I will take your place. You take my elephant,' he said. Sumant happily agreed and rode off on elephant back just before the soldiers arrived. They picked up the bag and threw it down the cliff.

The next day, Sumant came back into the city, seated on the elephant. He marched up to the king's court and in answer to everyone's surprised questions said, 'When I was thrown off the cliff I landed in a beautiful kingdom called Alakavati in the valley. Its streets are paved with gold and everyone has masses of gold and silver scattered all over their houses. But they have no king, and when I landed among them, after being thrown from the mountain, they decided to make me the king. Today is my coronation. Please come with me to Alakavati.'

The king heard the story in silence. Then he said, 'Sumant, you have told many stories in your life. But this one I will not believe. I know that valley well. There is no Alakavati there. Since you are so clever, why don't you use your wits for the betterment of this kingdom and not just for yourself?'

Sumant was silent. No one had praised him or offered him a better life ever before. He accepted the king's offer. He went on to study under the best pundits of the kingdom and one day was known all over the country as the wisest of the king's ministers.

## 21

## THE CASE OF THE MISSING NECKLACE

Princess Chandravati was very beautiful. She loved all kinds of jewellery and always wanted to wear the most precious, most lovely jewels. Once, a jeweller came to the palace and gifted the king a wonderful diamond necklace. It glittered with small and big diamonds. It was certainly a very expensive necklace. The princess fell in love with it as soon as she saw it, so the king presented it to her.

After that, the princess always wore the necklace, wherever she went. One day, she was walking in the palace garden when she felt like taking a dip in the pond. She took off the necklace and put it in the hands of her oldest and most trusted servant. 'Hold this,' she said, 'and be careful. This is the most precious necklace in the whole world.'

The servant, an old woman, settled down under a tree, holding tightly on to the ornament. But it was a hot summer afternoon and they had been walking for a while . . . Slowly the woman's eyes started closing and soon she was snoring gently. Just as she was drifting off into a wonderful dream, she felt someone tugging the necklace from her hands. She woke up with a start and looked around. There was no one, and the necklace was gone! Scared out of her wits, she started screaming. The royal guards rushed up and she pointed in the direction she thought the thief may have taken. The guards ran off that way.

Now who should be walking on that road, but a poor and slightly stupid farmer. As soon as he saw a platoon of the king's palace guards rushing down the road, thundering towards him, he thought they wanted to catch him and started running. But he was not a very strong man and could not outrun the hefty guards. They caught him in no time.

'Where is it?' they demanded, shaking him.

'Where is what?' he stammered back.

'The necklace you stole!' the guards shouted, giving him a few more shakes.

The farmer had no idea what they were talking about. He only understood something was lost and he was supposed to have it. 'I don't know where it is now,' he said quickly. 'I gave it to my landlord.'

The guards now ran to the landlord's house. 'Give

us the necklace!' they demanded of the fat landlord as he sat balancing his account books. 'Necklace!' The landlord was startled. 'I don't have any.'

'Then tell us quickly who does!'

The landlord saw the priest walking by the house. He pointed a chubby finger at him. 'He does! That man has it.' The guards now caught hold of the priest who was walking to the temple, thinking about the creamy payasam his wife had made for lunch. He was stunned when a pack of burly guards jumped on him and demanded a necklace. He remembered the minister Bhupati, who was at the temple now, praying to the goddess. He took the guards to the temple and pointed at the praying minister. 'I gave it to him.'

Bhupati too was caught and all four men were thrown into jail. Now, the chief minister of the kingdom knew Bhupati well. He was a good and honest man who had served the king faithfully for many years, so the chief minister was puzzled. Why had Bhupati suddenly stolen the princess's favourite ornament?

He decided to find out and asked one of his spies to listen to the men as they sat talking in the jail.

First Bhupati asked the priest, 'Why did you say you gave me a necklace? I was praying quietly in the temple, and you have landed me in jail.'

The priest scratched his head and pointed to the landlord. 'I didn't know what else to do. But *he* set the guards on me. I was only walking by his house.'

The landlord looked sheepish. Then he turned burning eyes on the farmer. 'You lazy good-for-nothing! Why did you say I had the necklace?'

The farmer, trembling under the angry gaze of the three men, said, 'The guards jumped on me so suddenly, I did not know what to say . . .'

When the spy reported this conversation to the chief minister, he understood that none of these men was the thief. So who was it? He ordered a thorough search of the palace garden, especially where the servant had sat dozing. The soldiers searched high and low, till they saw something glinting in the tree. There sat a huge monkey. And around its neck was the most beautiful, most precious necklace in the whole world!

Of course, it took a lot of coaxing and a huge bunch of bananas, before the monkey agreed to have the necklace removed from around its neck. And the princess decided the world's most expensive diamond necklace was best worn indoors!

## 22

## A QUESTION OF MATHS

Srimukha was a clever but poor farmer. One day, he learnt that the king was passing through the village and would be stopping there for a night. He decided to give the king a gift and perhaps earn a small reward. He took his best cock to the king and presented it to him.

The king was very pleased to get such a fine bird. Then he saw the intelligent look on Srimukha's face and decided to test him. 'In my family, I have a wife, two sons and two daughters, and you are my guest today. Tell me, how can I divide this one cock among seven people?'

Srimukha thought for a while and said, 'It is easy. You are the head of the family, so you should get the head. Your wife will get the cock's back as she is the backbone of the family. Your daughters will one day get married and go away, so they should get the two wings, and your sons will follow the path you show them, so they should get the legs.'

'And what about you?'

'I am the guest, so I should get whatever is left over.'

The king was pleased by this clever answer and presented Srimukha with a gold coin. Now Srimukha had a foolish neighbour, Sripati, who became very jealous when he heard about the reward. He decided to present the king with five cocks and earn five pieces of gold.

When he appeared before the king with the five cocks, the king asked him the same question. 'How can five cocks be divided between seven people?'

Sripati was dumbstruck. Who knew the king would ask such a difficult question? As he stood trying to calculate, the king sent for Srimukha. The farmer heard the question and quickly worked out the answer. 'We will divide everyone into groups of three,' he said. 'Your Majesty and the queen and one cock will be one group. So the king and queen will get one cock. The two princesses and one cock will be another group. The two princes and one cock will form the third group. I will form the last group with the remaining two cocks, so I will get two cocks.'

The king smiled delightedly at this answer. He presented Srimukha with some more gold coins and turned to Sripati who stood there open-mouthed, still counting on his fingers. 'The coins are rewards for Srimukha's intelligence, not the cocks,' he explained gently.

## 23

## THE CLEVER BROTHERS

Once upon a time, there were three brothers. They were all very clever and one day decided to make their fortune using their powers of reasoning and logic.

As they walked to the nearest big city to look for work, they saw some footprints on the dirt road. As they stood looking at the marks, a merchant came rushing up to them. 'Did you see anything go by on this road?' he asked in a panic. The first brother looked closely at the prints and said, 'Yes, a large camel.' The second said, 'It was a one-eyed camel.' The third, who had been looking further down the road, said, 'It was carrying a woman and a child on its back.'

Now the merchant was furious and shouted, 'You have kidnapped my wife and child. Come with me to the king.'

The three brothers could not get him to see reason and the four men ended up in the king's court. 'Hmm,' the king said, after he had heard the entire story. 'If you three claim to be so clever, let me set a task for you. I will place before you a wooden box which will be locked. You will have to tell me what contains it without looking inside.'

The three brothers agreed, and soon the king's men placed before them a stout wooden box, firmly shut. The first brother said immediately, 'It has something round inside.'

The second said, 'It is a pomegranate.'

'An unripe pomegranate,' added the third.

The box was opened and indeed, inside there was an unripe pomegranate.

The king now asked them for an explanation. The first man said, 'When your servant was bringing the box, I heard something rolling inside. That meant there was a round object in it.' The second man said, 'I saw your servant coming from the pomegranate orchard, so I knew he had placed a pomegranate in the box.'

'And this is not the season for pomegranates, so it had to be an unripe one,' piped up the last brother.

The king now had proof of the brothers' powers of observation and asked them how they knew about the merchant's wife and child being on camel back.

'The footprints we saw were large ones, so I deduced it was a big camel that had gone that way,' said the first brother.

'The camel had grazed on only one side of the road,' said the second, 'so I knew it was one-eyed.'

'And I saw the footprints of a woman and a child where the camel had sat down to rest,' said the third. 'Which meant they were on the camel's back.'

The king, now convinced of their cleverness, appointed the three brothers as ministers in his court.

## 24

## THE LUCKY PURSE

Mallika was the daughter of a rich widow. She was very beautiful and kind. When she got engaged to be married to the son of a rich landlord, her mother started making all sorts of preparations. She bought beautiful saris, lovely jewellery and all kinds of gifts for Mallika and her in-laws. Mallika wanted to put some of these gifts in a silk bag to take with her. So her faithful old servant Veda was sent to the market to buy one.

Veda returned with a bag, but Mallika did not like the design. So she sent Veda back to the shop to change it. Now, there was only one bag left, and even though it had a peculiar design and a very odd shape, Veda brought it back home. Of course Mallika did not like it one bit. However, she had no choice but to use it.

Soon Mallika got married and it was time for her to leave for her new house. It was in the next village, and her mother packed lots of food for the journey. She put it all in the odd-shaped silk bag. As Mallika was saying her goodbyes, her mother whispered in her ear, 'I have put lots of fruits, coconuts, flowers and some other gifts in the silk bag. Keep it carefully.' She also said something else, but Mallika's friends set up such a wailing then over their departing friend that she could not hear her mother's last few words.

There was a terrible thunderstorm that night and Mallika and the people accompanying her had to stop to take shelter in an old abandoned temple. There, as Mallika stood gazing out at the rain, she heard the sound of someone crying. She looked around and saw a girl, about her age, also dressed like a newly married bride, sitting and crying on the temple floor. Kind-hearted Mallika went up to her and asked what the matter was. Sobbing, the girl told her that she was an orphan. She had just been married off by her uncle who had looked after her all these years. But he was too poor and had not been able to give her any gifts to give to her new family. Now she was worried about what her in-laws would have to say. Mallika felt sad when she heard the story. Then her eyes fell on the peculiar silk bag her mother had given her. It was full of fruits and flowers. Mallika picked it up and gave it to the girl. By then, the storm had died down, and the two brides went their different ways.

Mallika soon got accustomed in her new house. She had a son and was happy with her husband who loved her dearly. Ten years went by, till one day, disaster struck. There was a severe earthquake. Mallika was outside, inspecting the field, so she was unhurt. But her husband and son could not be found anywhere. Almost mad with grief, Mallika started wandering in search of them. Her beautiful house was nothing but a pile of bricks now. Her wealth was gone. Her whole life had been destroyed all of a sudden.

She went from village to village. There were many people like her, homeless and hungry, walking about. Then she heard that in the next town there was a wealthy couple who had built some rooms to shelter people like her and also gave them food. She decided to go there.

When she reached the place, she saw there was a long queue of people waiting for food. Not having eaten a morsel for many days, she joined them. Many more people joined the queue behind her. But as soon as the man distributing the food gave her her portion, he announced the food was finished for the day. The people behind her had to go away empty-handed. Just as Mallika was about to start eating, she noticed a tired old woman sitting by the roadside, watching her. The woman had obviously not eaten in many days. Without thinking twice, Mallika gave her portion to the woman.

The man distributing the food saw this. That night, when he was telling the woman who had donated the food about the events of the day, he mentioned Mallika and her generosity. The woman, Soudamani, was touched. 'Bring her to me,' she said. 'My little son needs someone to look after him, and I want someone who is honest and kind-hearted.'

So Mallika started living with the couple. She loved the boy like her own. Indeed, he was exactly her son's age and she would often think of her past life and lost family and shed tears. Soudamani would console her and soon the two women became friends.

Mallika was allowed to take the child to any part of the house except for the prayer room. That was always kept locked and only Soudamani and her husband went in there to offer their prayers. When Mallika asked Soudamani, she said, 'Don't bring the child there. We have kept something very precious to us in the room and we don't want him spoiling anything.'

One day, when Mallika and the boy were playing ball, the child threw the ball hard and it sailed through a window and landed in the prayer room. The boy started crying; he wanted the ball right then. Mallika tried her best to make him understand but he would not listen. Unable to bear his crying, Mallika decided to get the ball, even if it meant disobeying her mistress.

She entered the room and was surprised to see that

instead of a deity, the only thing in the room was a peculiar silk bag! She recognized it immediately as the one she had given to the orphan girl the night she had left for her new home. Old memories rushed up and she started crying. Just then, Soudamani entered the room and was furious to see Mallika there.

'Why did you touch that purse? I told you never to come in here,' shouted Soudamini.

'This is my purse,' Mallika answered in tears. 'I had given it to an orphan girl one night, when I was on my way to my in-laws' house for the first time.'

'When did you get married?' Soudamini asked, her anger dying down.

'Ten years ago, in the month of Shravan.'

Hearing this, Soudamini too burst into tears. She came and hugged Mallika. 'I was that girl. Perhaps you did not know it when you gave the purse to me, but along with the fruits, it also contained several diamonds and coins. I opened the bag only after I reached home. We tried to find you and tell you, but we did not even know your name. We became rich with your gift but never forgot how you helped a poor orphan girl in her time of need. We kept the bag in the prayer room and used it to remind us every day of your generosity and kindness. That is why we decided to help others when we were no longer poor. Whatever we have today is also yours.'

Mallika and Soudamani became even better friends

after this. They sent out people to look for Mallika's family and one day, to her great joy, she was reunited with her lost son and husband.

## 25

# Two Unforgettable Lessons!

Amrutananda and Kapiladeva were landlords in neighbouring villages. Both were cunning and extremely sly. They had made a lot of money by cheating and ill-treating their labourers who worked in the fields.

One day, a young man named Manikya came to Amrutananda, asking for work. Amrutananda was pleasantly surprised. No one ever wanted to work for him because of his reputation, and here was someone walking right into his house! Manikya's next few words got him even more excited. Manikya said, 'I will work for you for free. You need not pay me a salary. Only give me a place to sleep, two sets of clothes and two meals a day.' Amrutananda was beside himself with joy when he heard this and was about to agree, when

Manikya added, 'I have only one condition: I will tell you the truth always, but one day in the year, I will tell lies.'

Amrutananda, who lied happily every day of the year, agreed to this odd condition. So Manikya joined him. He was a wonderful worker—hard-working and trustworthy. He was very honest and soon became Amrutananda's right-hand man.

A year went by. Because of Manikya's hard work, Amrutananda had an excellent harvest. He and his wife, Mandakini, decided to have a big feast to celebrate. They invited all their relatives and friends, who gathered from all over the village and outside too. Everyone was looking forward to the delicious feast being planned. On the morning of the feast, Amrutananda decided he would also give away some gifts to his relatives, just to show off. So he set off for the market in his cart. As soon as he was out of sight, Manikya went running to his mistress, Mandakini. He wept loudly and beat his chest. Then he fell on the floor, sobbing, and announced, 'The master is dead! The cart overturned on the road. Our master has been flattened like a chapatti!' As soon as Amrutananda's wife and relatives heard this, they started wailing. Manikya rushed out, saying he would bring back the body, while everyone started preparing for the last rites.

Manikya now went running to his master and said, 'Master! Your wife is dead. My kind, loving mistress is dead. A cobra bit her and she fell to the ground, as blue as the spring sky.' Amrutananda was stunned. What! His beloved Mandakini, his partner in all his schemes, was dead! He rushed back home shouting her name.

Mandakini too was weeping loudly, sitting in the courtyard. When she saw her husband run in, she stopped mid-wail, and Amrutananda too stood open-mouthed. Then they fell into each other's arms, unable to believe their eyes.

As one, they turned to Manikya. 'What is the meaning of this, Manikya?' his master demanded to know, sternly.

Manikya smiled. 'Remember my condition, that I would lie only one day in the year? Well, I chose today. You see what lies can do? They nearly destroyed your life. Now think what happens to the people to whom you lie every day of the year!'

Saying this, he walked out, leaving behind a stunned and ashamed landlord.

Manikya walked to the next village now, to Kapiladeva's house. Kapiladeva had heard all about him and was ready with his own conditions.

'You will not lie, ever,' he said. 'And you cannot leave the farm. If you do, you will have to pay me ten gold coins. If I want to get rid of you, I will give you five coins. In return you will be given clothes, shelter and one leaf-plate filled with food every day.'

Manikya thought for a while, then agreed. He began

his work, and at the end of the day, stood waiting for his leaf full of food. The cook came and handed him a tiny leaf on which there were a few grains of rice. Quickly Manikya produced a large banana leaf. 'The master did not say what kind of leaf. I want this leaf to be piled up with food. That was the agreement.' The cook had no choice but to fill Manikya's banana leaf-plate with rice, dal and three types of vegetables. Manikya took it and had a hearty meal, which he did not forget to share with the other labourers, his new friends.

This went on for a few days. Manikya was not at all interested in working. All day he would sit around with the other workers, telling them also to while away time chatting, and at the end of the day he would tuck into a big meal. Word soon reached Kapiladeva and he decided to teach Manikya a lesson.

'Manikya, I want you to change the direction of the river so that it passes through my garden,' he ordered. Then he left, happy that Manikya would never be able to do this and would have to leave, after paying him ten gold coins.

When he came home in the evening, he was horrified to see the front wall and the front door of his house lying in pieces. 'Manikya!' he shouted angrily. 'What is the meaning of this?'

Manikya appeared, wiping his brow. 'Why, I am making way for the river to enter the garden. Now I will go to the river and ask it to come this way.'

Kapiladeva sat clutching his head. Manikya had got the better of him again!

The next day, he summoned Manikya and, just to keep him out of mischief, ordered, 'Bring me the wood from twenty trees.' That would keep him busy for the day, going to the forest and doing all the chopping, he thought.

Manikya picked up the axe, and whistling happily, proceeded to chop down the prized mango trees in Kapiladeva's orchard! When he returned, Kapiladeva had to admit that Manikya was too expensive to keep and happily paid him ten gold coins so that he would leave, and never come back again!

That was how Manikya taught the two meanest landlords in the land lessons they would never forget!

## 26

## UNITED WE STAND

Maruti and Mahadeva lived in the same village. While Mahadeva was a rich businessman and owned the largest shop in the village, Maruti was a poor farmer. Both had large families, with many sons, daughters-in-law and grandchildren.

One day, Maruti, tired of not being able to make ends meet, decided to leave the village and move to the city with his family. There they were sure to earn enough to feed everyone. They said their goodbyes, packed their few clothes and set off.

When night fell, they stopped and rest under a large tree. There was a stream running nearby, where they could get a drink and refresh themselves. Maruti looked around and started giving instructions to everyone. He called his sons and told them to clean the area below the tree. He told his wife to fetch water. He instructed his daughters-in-law to make the fire and himself started cutting wood from the tree. Now, on the top of that tree sat a thief, resting with his booty. He watched as Maruti's family worked together to prepare dinner. He also noticed they had nothing to cook—no grains or vegetables.

Maruti's wife too must have thought the same thing, for she came to her husband as he sat resting under the tree and said, 'Everything is ready. Now what shall we cook?' Maruti raised his hands upwards and said, 'Don't worry. He is watching all this from above. He will help us.'

'But how will he help us?'

'We are many. We are united. He will come down for us.'

The thief got worried. He had seen that the family was a large one and they worked well together. They listened to each other and were obedient to the old man. Surely they did not know he was hiding in the branches? Were they waiting for him to come down? He decided to make a quick getaway. He climbed down swiftly when they were not looking and ran for his life. Unfortunately, he forgot his bundle of stolen jewels and money, which dropped down into Maruti's lap. He opened it and jumped with joy when he saw what it contained. 'Come here, quick!' he called out. 'See, I was right. I knew God above would look after us, and He has thrown down this bundle for us. Now our days of want are over. Let us go back to the village.'

So the family gathered its belongings and returned to the village. There was great excitement when they told everyone the story of how they got rich.

Fat old Mahadeva got greedy. This was a nice quick way to earn some money! So he commanded his family to pack some clothes and they set off as if on a journey. They stopped under the same tree and Mahadeva started commanding everyone just like Maruti had done. But the difference was that no one in his family was willing to listen to anyone or obey orders. They were used to having a bunch of servants wait on them. So the one who went to the river to fetch water had a nice bath and came back. The person who went to gather wood for the fire went off to sleep beneath the tree. And Mahadeva only ordered everyone about, not bothering to do anything himself.

The thief had returned to his treetop. He sat there sadly, thinking of his lost bundle and watching the family underneath. He noticed the family members were greedy and selfish. They would never be able to put up a fight together, he was sure.

Then, Mahadeva and his wife started the conversation which they had rehearsed many times carefully.

Mahadeva's wife said, 'Everything is ready. Now what shall we cook?' Mahadeva raised his hands upwards and said, 'Don't worry. He is watching all this from above. He will help us.'

'But how will he help us?'

'We are many. We are united. He will come down for us.'

At this the thief jumped down from the top of the tree, a knife in his hand. Seeing him, everyone was scared and started running in different directions to save themselves. They started screaming and no one would help the other.

The thief stole everything. Mahadeva's wife's necklace and earrings, the greedy old man's pouch full of money, hidden under his fat tummy.

Mahadeva and his family returned to the village empty-handed, having lost all that they had taken with them.

## 27

## WHERE DID IT GO?

Once upon a time, there was a shrewd shopkeeper called Makarand. He had a friend called Mihir, who had saved a lot of money. Mihir was keen to go on a pilgrimage, but he did not know where to leave his precious savings. So he came to Makarand's shop and said, 'Friend, I trust you more than anyone. Please look after my life's savings till I return from my pilgrimage.'

Makarand pretended to think seriously, then said, 'No. Money spoils relationships. What if something happens to it when you are not here? You will no longer be my friend.'

As Mihir stood there thinking about this, an old woman entered the shop and bought some things. One of the boys helping Makarand gave her less change than he should have. Makarand saw this and pretended to scold the boy, then ordered him to return the remaining money to the woman.

Mihir, not knowing this was an act put up by Makarand to make him believe in his honesty, was convinced. 'I have decided. I will leave the money only with you.'

Makarand smiled. 'Then let us do something. Let's take the bag of coins and bury it in a place about which only you and I will know. That way, even if something happens to me when you are gone, you will know where your money is.'

Simple Mihir thought this was a good idea and the two went and hid the bag in a secret place. Mihir left the next day on his pilgrimage, happy his savings were in safe hands. Six months later, Mihir returned. He dumped his luggage at home and went to dig out his bag. But even though he searched and searched, there was no sign of the bag anywhere.

In panic, he ran to Makarand, who was busy in his shop. When Mihir asked him about the bag, Makarand pretended to be surprised. 'But I did not even go that way in all these months. Why don't you search for it again?' he said, putting on his most innocent look. Mihir had no choice but to believe him. Sadly, he made his way home.

On the way, who should he meet but the old woman he had seen in Makarand's shop. Seeing his sad face, she asked him what the matter was. Mihir told her the whole story. Then she smiled and whispered a plan to him.

Not long after, the woman came to Makarand's shop, carrying a big box. 'Brother, I heard you are a good and honest man. My son went on pilgrimage many months ago and has still not returned. I am worried and have decided to go look for him. Will you look after my box of two hundred gold coins while I am away?'

Makarand could not believe his luck. He was about to launch into his idea about hiding the box, when an angry Mihir entered the shop. 'Where is . . .' But before he could complete his sentence, Makarand, afraid of being accused in front of the old woman, said quickly, 'I forgot. I had seen some pigs digging around there and had removed the bag just to keep it safe. Here it is.' And he handed Mihir the bag he had stolen many months back.

Now the old woman pretended she was seeing Mihir for the first time. 'Son, did you also go on a pilgrimage? Tell me, did you meet my son anywhere?'

Mihir, clutching his precious bag, said, 'Yes, Auntie. I met him on the road a few villages away. He was on his way home. He should be here in a week.'

The old woman leaned over and took her box away from Makarand. 'Thank you, son, you have saved me an unnecessary trip. Now I will need some money to prepare for my son's welcome,' she added to Mihir.

And the two left the shop, holding their boxes. Makarand could only stare at them open-mouthed.

## 28

## The Princess Who Was a Bird

Long ago, there lived a beautiful princess. When she grew into a lovely young woman, her father wanted her to get married. In fact, there was a long queue of princes eager to marry her. But the princess would not even look at them. She would not have anything to do with a man apart from her father, she declared.

The poor king was puzzled and wondered what had happened for her to hate men so much. He tried pleading and begging and commanding, but the princess was firm. In the meantime, the entire kingdom had come to know about the princess's refusal to get married, and the people could talk of nothing else.

One day, a handsome prince from a neighbouring kingdom heard about the princess and was curious. He wanted to see this princess famous for her beauty and perhaps convince her to marry him. So he disguised himself as an ordinary young man and came to her kingdom. He stopped at an inn for the night, where he hoped to meet someone who could tell him the story of the princess who hated men. Then he got lucky. He happened to meet a woman who took flowers to the palace every day for the princess's garlands.

He chatted with the old woman for a long time and found out the entire story. The princess had lost her mother when she was a little girl. She had been brought up by a nurse. This nurse would tell her a story every day. The story was about a pair of myna birds that lived in a nest in a thick forest. They had many beautiful chicks and were proud of their neat little nest. They were also deeply in love with each other. But one day, a fierce fire started in the forest and the flames started climbing towards their nest. 'Let us take our chicks and flee,' the female myna told her husband, but he would not hear of it. 'There's nothing to worry,' he said. 'I will look after you all.' The flames came closer and closer and the female myna kept begging her husband to save their chicks, but he told her to relax and did nothing. When finally the fire reached the tree and started licking at the nest and the wife was getting charred with her babies, she saw her husband fly away, leaving them to die.

The princess would ask her nurse to tell her this story every day, and after a while began to believe she had been the female myna in her previous life. So, in this life, she did not want to trust any man or get married.

The prince thought hard all night and decided what he would do next. As soon as it was morning, he arrived at the king's palace. There he demanded an audience with the king. He introduced himself as a storyteller. 'I have travelled many lands and know many stories,' he said loudly. 'I can tell you wonderful tales from all over the world. My only condition is, I will not talk to a woman.' The king was surprised. 'Why do you say such a thing?' he asked. By then the prince saw that the princess too had arrived in the court and was listening to him from behind a screen.

He cleared his throat and said, 'That is the oddest tale in my collection. During my wanderings, I met a sage. I served him for many days and he became very pleased with me. One day, happy with my devotion, he told me the story of my previous life. I was a male myna then. I used to live in a thick green forest with my myna wife and our little chicks. One day, there was a fire and the flames started creeping up towards our tree. I told my wife, "Let us go from here," but she would not listen. "There is enough time," she said to me. When finally the fire reached the nest and began to burn me and the chicks, I saw my wife fly away and save herself, leaving us to die. Ever since I heard that story I have hated women and have decided not to talk with, let alone marry one.'

When she heard this, the princess pushed aside the screen and appeared before the prince, her eyes blazing with anger. 'How dare you!' she shouted. '*I* was the one who wanted to save everyone and *you* were the one who left us to die. I was that female myna in my previous life.' But the prince argued back, 'It was not you but I who died in that fire.'

The argument carried on for a while. Finally the king managed to get a word in. 'Stop, stop!' he commanded. 'No fighting in court! Perhaps you two were married to each other in your previous lives. And perhaps something did happen which made one of you leave in a time of need. Now you must understand that friends and partners always stay together. When something goes wrong, they help each other. Why don't you two get married in this life too, and see if you can help one another, in good times and bad, like the best of friends, and make up for the mistakes of your past lives?'

The prince and princess stopped shouting long enough to take a good look at each other and think over these words. The princess saw the prince's intelligent and kind eyes. She decided to heed her father's advice and the two got married soon after. And yes, they lived happily for many, many years, through good times and bad, like best friends.

## 29

# THE PRICE IS RIGHT

Somendra was a cunning merchant. He was ready to do anything to earn some money. No one knew what trick he would be up to next. Nandish was a simple village boy. He was poor and had nothing in the world but one beautiful white horse. He loved it more than anything else. Everyone in the village knew about him and the horse. Somendra had had his eye on the horse for a long time and was always trying to think of a way to get it for himself.

One day, Nandish rode his horse to the village fair. On his way back, he met Somendra. The crafty merchant thought, 'Nandish is a simpleton. Let me see if I can trick him out of his horse.'

So he said to Nandish, 'You live all alone. How do you manage? You must be in great need of money always. I have an idea. What does a young boy like you need with a horse? Sell it to me and I'll make you rich in return.'

Nandish replied, 'No. I don't want to sell the horse.'

But Somendra was not one to give up so easily. He followed Nandish, offering him more and more money. Finally, when the offer reached five hundred gold coins, Nandish paused and seemed to give it a thought. Then he said, 'Five hundred gold coins seems like a good price. But I have a condition. If you agree to that, I will give you my horse.'

By now Somendra would have agreed to anything. 'What is it? Tell me,' he said impatiently. Nandish said, 'You must give me the money right now, and I will give you the horse only when I have given you ten lashes.'

'That's all!' exclaimed Somendra. Ten lashes was nothing. He would resell the horse for over a thousand coins in the market. Why, he was ready to take twenty lashes to make such a profit. He agreed instantly. Then he ran home and got the money for Nandish. He also brought a whip for Nandish to lash him with. Nandish counted the coins carefully. Then he took the whip. One, two, three . . . the lashes fell on Somendra's back in quick succession. By the eighth lash he was ready to cry, but he told himself, only two more and the horse would be his. He had dreamt of buying it for so long. Nine . . . Somendra waited, holding his breath for the last and final lash. But what was this! Nandish had mounted his horse and was riding off, merrily throwing the whip on the ground!

'Wait!' shouted Somendra in anger. 'What about the tenth lash? And where are you taking the horse? We had a deal.'

Nandish stopped and said, 'I agreed to give you the horse only after I have given you ten lashes. Now I don't feel like giving you the last one. It upsets my dear horse. I'll give it to you only when I am in the mood. Till then, goodbye!'

'Come back, you cheat!' screamed Somendra. But the crowd that had gathered around him agreed. A deal was a deal. Nandish could give the tenth and final lash whenever he wanted, and till then the horse could not belong to Somendra.

Nandish rode away, richer by five hundred gold coins. Somendra waited for many, many days for the whip to fall on his back finally. Of course, it never came!

## 30

# A Lesson for the Uncles

Rajendra was a young boy who had lost both his parents when he was still quite young. He lived all by himself. He had one goat with which he stayed in a tiny hut. He also had three uncles, who were always trying to cheat him out of his goat and house. They made his life miserable.

One day, the uncles stole his goat and tied it alongside some other goats that belonged to the village butcher. Poor Rajendra looked everywhere for it. The butcher, meanwhile, took all the goats and killed them for their meat. Now, Rajendra's goat wore a special bell around its neck. When the butcher cut that goat, he threw away the bell. Rajendra found it soon after and was grief-stricken. He knocked on the butcher's door for justice. By then the butcher had realized that he had killed

Rajendra's goat. Scared that the boy would tell everyone he had killed a stolen goat, he gave Rajendra some money and sent him away.

When the uncles saw their nephew coming home with the coins jingling in his pocket, they were astonished. How had Rajendra made money from a lost goat? When they asked him he said, 'Everyone wanted goat's meat today in the market. My poor goat somehow ended up at the butcher's and he sold its meat and made a lot of money. This is my share.'

The uncles thought this was a good way to make money. They owned twenty goats and they slaughtered them all and went to the market to sell the meat. But now there was so much meat in the market that the prices had come down and they got only a few rupees for their goats.

Angry at being fooled, they decided to burn down Rajendra's hut. So one day, when Rajendra had gone out, they set fire to his little hut. The young boy was shocked to come home and find a pile of smouldering ash where his hut used to be. At once he knew who was behind it. Sadly he gathered the ash in a bag and decided to leave the village forever. With the bag slung over his shoulder, he set off. After walking for many miles, he at last reached a village. He sat down under a tree to rest and think what to do next.

Soon a crowd of curious villagers gathered around him. Who was this stranger? Why was he carrying a bag of ashes, they wondered. Finally one man asked him, 'What is the matter? Why are you sitting quietly like this? Why are you carrying so much ash?'

Rajendra's hut had been his dearest, most sacred possession, so he said, 'It is the ash from a sacred place.'

Now the villagers were excited. 'Will you sell it to us?' they asked.

'No.'

But they would not give up. 'Give us a pinch at least,' they begged. Rajendra agreed and gave them a pinch of ash each. Soon, word spread in the village that a holy man had come from the Himalayas, who looked like he was twenty but was really eighty years old. He was carrying a bag of ashes with him that could cure all misfortunes and disease. He was giving away a pinch of it only to each person, and though he wanted no money, it was only right that you paid a coin at least for such happiness.

Thus a long queue formed in front of Rajendra. Each villager took a pinch of ash and left a coin in return. At the end of the day, Rajendra discovered the ash was all gone and in its place he had a pile of coins.

Happily, he decided to go back to his village and start life afresh. When he came back, his uncles could not believe their eyes. How had Rajendra done this? They asked Rajendra his secret. Rajendra said, 'There is a great demand for the ashes in that village. I sold the ash that I gathered from my burnt hut and got all this money.' The uncles were amazed. If Rajendra could get so much money by selling the ash from his little hut, how much would they get if they burnt their sprawling houses and sold the ash? That night itself, they burnt down their houses, gathered the ashes in huge sacks and set off for the village. But as soon as they reached and uttered the word 'ash', why, all the villagers fell on them and beat them black and blue! By then the villagers knew there was no magic in the ash. And here were three more people trying to fool them!

The uncles somehow saved their skins and ran home. They were even angrier with Rajendra now for having tricked them a second time. They decided to kill him. One day, they invited him for a walk with them by the river. As they stood on the bridge, where the river was at its deepest, one of them pointed at the water and exclaimed, 'See! A beautiful mermaid!'

As soon as Rajendra leaned over to look in, they pushed him from behind and ran home. Poor Rajendra nearly drowned. Just in time, a girl washing clothes nearby heard his screams for help and dived in. She was a good swimmer and saved his life.

A grateful Rajendra told her the story of his life. She thought for a while and then whispered a plan in his ear.

The next day Rajendra arrived at his uncles' house. With him was the girl, dressed in beautiful clothes and jewellery. Rajendra also held a bag in his hands. His uncles were astonished to see him alive. How had he survived? Rajendra said, 'When I fell into the river, this beautiful girl saved me. She has a palace at the bottom of the river. She fell in love with me and married me. She also gave me half her riches. Now we will live in the river. Do come and visit us some time.' Saying this, they left in the direction of the river. The uncles had a quick discussion and decided they would follow Rajendra to his palace in the river and perhaps cheat him of his newfound wealth. So they ran to the river and dived into its deep waters.

They were never heard of again.

## 31

## A BAG OF WORDS

Keerti Kumara was a handsome young shepherd. He could play the flute wonderfully. Whenever he played on his simple bamboo flute, which he had made with his own hands, his sheep would listen to it spellbound and do whatever he wanted them to.

The princess of that kingdom was very beautiful. Her father, the king, wanted her to choose a prince and marry him, but she found fault with all the suitors he brought to her. They were so dull, they bored her to tears. Finally, she set an unusual condition. 'I will marry only that man who will be able to look after our hundred rabbits for a month, without losing a single one.'

Soon word of this strange condition spread in the kingdom. Keerti too heard it and decided to give it a try. He landed up at the king's palace, clutching his flute. The king and queen were shocked that a scruffy shepherd wanted to marry their daughter, but they had to keep their word, and Keerti was shown the cage with the hundred rabbits.

The next morning, Keerti went to the cage and, blowing softly into his flute, he led the rabbits to a beautiful meadow where they played, grazed and listened to the music. Not one rabbit tried to escape, and the predators like eagles and foxes too kept away.

The princess heard about this strange and exciting suitor and decided to see him for herself. She went to the meadow and instantly fell in love with the handsome boy who played such divine music. She started meeting him every day. When the king and queen heard about this, they were furious. Not only was the boy fulfilling the condition, the princess too supported him! How could their beautiful daughter marry a poor shepherd!

One day, as Keerti lay on the soft grass with the rabbits hopping about him, a stranger approached him. 'Give me a rabbit and I will give you a gold bar,' said the man. Keerti of course understood that this was no one but the king in disguise. He jumped up and said, 'Of course you can have a rabbit, but first you must wash my dirty clothes, massage my feet and polish my shoes. Then I will give you a rabbit.'

The king had no choice but to do all this. He was only happy no one saw him. Then he took a rabbit, popped it into a sack and walked back to the palace quickly. Keerti gathered the rest of the rabbits and took them home, softly playing his flute. As soon as the king reached the palace, the queen came out to greet him. Joyfully, he opened the sack to show her the rabbit. In a flash, the rabbit leapt out of the bag and hopped off to join its friends, who had followed the king to the palace with Keerti.

Furious, the queen now decided *she* would get a rabbit. A few days later, again Keerti was lying on the grass when an old woman came up to him and asked for a rabbit. She promised him two bars of gold for it. Keerti knew it was the queen and said, 'Of course you can have the rabbit. But first you must cook food for me, stitch my torn clothes and cut my hair, then you can have one of my rabbits.'

The queen reluctantly agreed to do all this and soon left with a rabbit in her bag. When she reached the palace, she first went into her room, carefully closed all the doors and windows, and then showed the rabbit to the king. Delighted that they had at last fooled the shepherd, the king flung open a window and yelled to the cook to make a delicious dinner to celebrate. Instantly the rabbit leapt out and hopped off to Keerti, who was standing outside the window, playing his flute.

One month passed and Keerti came to the palace to

claim the princess's hand. But the queen spoke up this time. 'You may have carried out my daughter's wish, but in order to marry her, you need to fulfil my wish too.'

Keerti had to agree. The queen commanded three sacks to be brought in. Then she said, 'Now fill these sacks with your words.'

Keerti thought for a while, then he picked up a sack and, holding it near his mouth, said, 'This is a true story. Once upon a time there was a mighty king. The whole kingdom trembled at his words. But one day he met a poor shepherd boy who made him wash his clothes, massage his dirty feet and polish his shoes . . .'

Immediately the king shouted, 'Enough, stop! The bag is full.'

'But my story is not over yet,' Keerti protested.

'Yes, it is. The bag is full,' said the king.

So Keerti picked up the second bag. He held it to his mouth and said, 'Once upon a time there was a beautiful queen. The king listened to every word she said. But one day she went to a poor shepherd boy and stitched his torn clothes, cut his hair . . .'

'Stop! Stop!' the queen shouted and tied the second bag.

Keerti Kumara opened the third bag. 'Once there was a lovely princess who fell in love with a poor shepherd boy. She would come up to the hills to meet him and . . .'

Now the king and the queen together tied the third bag. They knew who the princess was and realized she had made a good choice in deciding to marry this clever, musical shepherd boy.

## 32

## MAGIC IN THE AIR

Sheelavati and Jayasheel were a poor old couple. Their only precious possession was one cow. Once, Jayasheel fell very sick. Soon all their money was used up in buying medicines and they realized they would have to sell the cow. Sheelavati would have to go to the market. She was a very simple woman, so her husband warned her, 'Don't talk to anyone. Just walk to the market, sell the cow and come back with the money.'

Sheelavati set off, leading the cow by a rope. On the way, she met four young men. They were the local thugs and enjoyed bullying and tormenting old people. When they saw Sheelavati with her cow, they decided to play a trick. One of them sneaked up behind her, untied the cow and tied a goat in its place. Sheelavati had been walking immersed in thought, worried about Jayasheel.

She was surprised when she heard a goat bleating behind her. It was true: her cow had vanished and she was holding a goat!

The four boys came up to her and said, 'There is some magic in the air these days. It turned your cow into a goat.'

Poor Sheelavati walked on with the goat. After a while, the boys untied the goat and tied a cock in its place. 'Cock-a-doodle-do,' crowed the cock and Sheelavati was surprised again. Now the goat had become a cock!

The four boys again shouted, 'Magic in the air, Grandma.'

Sheelavati now walked on with the cock. The boys crept up again and tied a log of wood in place of the cock. Sheelavati was surprised to hear the sound of wood dragging on the road behind her. 'Magic in the air, Grandma,' shouted the boys again.

Then, as she dragged the wood, the boys untied that too and ran away. When Sheelavati reached the market, she found she was holding only a rope in her hand. Feeling sad, she came back home. She had lost the cow and not got any money either. When she told Jayasheel the story of the magic, he knew what had happened. He told his wife, 'Tomorrow make chapatti, vegetable and kheer for lunch. Make sure you cook for four people. I will come home with some guests. As soon as they come, you must say, "I cooked what the rabbit told me. Come, eat your lunch." Leave everything else to me.'

The next morning, Jayasheel went and borrowed two identical rabbits from a friend. He left one at home and tied the other with a string and started walking towards the market with it. On the way, he too met the four thugs. 'Hey, Grandfather!' they yelled. 'Your wife's cow vanished yesterday. Where are you taking this rabbit now?'

Jayasheel sighed sadly and said, 'This rabbit is like my son. It obeys my every word. But now I am sick and we need money, so I am having to sell it in the market.'

The four were surprised when they heard this. 'Does it really understand what you say, Grandfather?' they asked.

'Of course it does. Here, watch me.' Jayasheel turned to the rabbit and said, 'Hop home, little one, and tell your mother to make chapatti, vegetable and kheer for four people.' Then he untied the string and let the rabbit hop away. He said to the boys, 'Come home and have lunch with me.'

When they reached Jayasheel's house, his wife welcomed them and said, 'I cooked what the rabbit told me. Come, eat your lunch.' And she laid out chapatti, vegetable and kheer for each of them. What was more, they saw the rabbit sitting in a corner of the room, tucking into a green leaf!

They were amazed and told Jayasheel, 'We will buy your rabbit.'

Jayasheel pretended to think, then said, 'It is very precious to me. How can I sell it?' When the four begged him and offered more and more money, he reluctantly agreed. They dropped a heap of coins in his hand and rushed away with the rabbit.

Now, the thugs had been blackmailing the landlord for some money. They said to the rabbit, 'Go tell the landlord to come and give us our money in ten minutes.'

The rabbit hopped off and they waited for the landlord. An hour went by, but there was no sign of him. They marched to his house, knocked loudly on the door and demanded, 'Give us our money and the rabbit.'

The furious landlord ordered his largest bodyguard to give them the thrashing of their lives.

Bleeding and bruised, the four went back to Jayasheel. 'You fooled us!' they shouted. 'Give us back our money at once.'

'There is magic in the air,' sighed Jayasheel. 'The money has disappeared!'

## 33

## THE SELFISH GROOM

Dhanagupta, a famous and rich merchant, had only one son, Yashodhana. The child was born when his father was already quite old, and being the only child, was brought up with great care. When he became a young man, his father started thinking about his marriage. But Yashodhana told him, 'I will choose my own bride. I want someone who is intelligent. She should also be careful with money, and not a spendthrift. After all, she will become the wife of a merchant with a vast business one day. Please give me a chariot, a servant and four horses. I will travel around the country and find such a wife for myself.'

His father agreed and gave him the chariot, servant and horses. Thus, Yashodhana set off to look for a bride. He travelled all over the country, met many women and their hopeful fathers. But whenever a beautiful woman appeared before him, he would say, 'I will marry you, but first take this bag of paddy. I want you to cook me a meal of rice, dal, vegetables and curd with this. Only if you do this will I marry you.'

Whoever heard this strange condition went away without trying. A few tried, but could not succeed. In this way many months went by and a weary Yashodhana arrived with his equally tired servant and horses at a small village. There he saw a small but neat hut, and sitting in front of it an old man and his daughter. The girl was beautiful, with dark, intelligent eyes. Yashodhana was suddenly hopeful. He went up to them and told them about his condition. The girl smiled when she heard him and said, 'Of course I can do it. It is not difficult. Why don't you rest awhile and I will get your meal ready.'

An astonished Yashodhana settled down to wait. Soon he nodded off to sleep. After some time, he felt someone shaking him awake. It was the girl, inviting him to lunch. He washed his hands and sat down. To his amazement, the girl served him fluffy white rice, two types of vegetables, a bowl of steaming-hot, delicious dal and soft, refreshing curd. He ate the meal and then could not hold back his curiosity any longer. 'How did you do it?' he asked.

The girl smiled. 'First I pounded the paddy and got a lot of rice. Then I took the husk to the village jeweller who needs it for his work. He gave me money in return, with which I bought the vegetables and the oil. Then, since there was more rice than could be eaten by one person, I sold the rest and got the curd and some ghee. It took me little time to cook it all and then your meal was ready.'

Yashodhana was amazed. Quickly he revealed who he was—the son of the country's richest man. But the girl was not impressed. She stood back, folded her arms, looked him in the eye and said, 'You may want to marry me, but I don't want to marry you. Look at the state of your horses and your poor servant. Did you think about them and feed them properly when you were travelling? I think not. You asked me to cook only for you. What about them? You need to learn some manners and kindness before you can even think of marrying me.'

An ashamed Yashodhana went back home empty-handed. Over the next few months he mended his ways, and one day arrived at the girl's hut, on foot. There, he humbly asked her father for her hand. The girl looked at his face, now shorn of arrogance. She also noticed the love in his gaze, and agreed.

Yashodhana and his wife looked after their large business with intelligence, compassion and honesty for many, many years.

## 34

## THE TIRED HORSE

Purushottam was a poor farmer. He lived in a village with his young son and a horse. They had never gone anywhere outside the village and were very simple people. One day, they decided to go to the grand fair that was on in the nearest town.

They set off early one morning. Purushottam thought his son was young and would not be able to walk the distance, so he made the lad sit on the horse and started walking beside it. When they had gone some distance, they passed a group of villagers. 'Look!' the villagers shouted. 'The young boy is sitting on the horse while his old father is walking. Hey, don't you have any brains? Let your father sit on the horse.'

Purushottam and his son thought this was right. So Purushottam sat on the horse and his son walked alongside. After a while they met another group of villagers. 'Look!' the villagers shouted. 'The man is sitting on the horse while the little boy is walking. Hey, don't you have any brains? Let your son sit on the horse.'

So Purushottam got off the horse, and not knowing what to do, the two walked beside the horse. Soon they met another group of villagers. 'Look!' the villagers shouted. 'There is a strong and healthy horse but they are walking on foot. Hey, don't you have any brains? Why don't you sit on the horse?'

Now they decided to both sit on the horse. A while later, they passed some more people. 'Look!' they shouted. 'Those two cruel people are sitting on that one poor animal. The horse looks tired. Hey! Why don't you both get off and carry the horse on your shoulders instead?'

Purushottam and his son got off. They used a rope to tie the horse's legs and, lifting it over their shoulders, started walking. They came to a stream. By then the horse was furious at being carried like this. As soon as the man and the boy set it down, it struggled out of the rope and ran away, never to be seen again.

## 35

## A Minister's Test

Long ago, there was a king who ruled his kingdom with great wisdom. He made sure each person got a good education and as a result, the people of the kingdom too were clever and wise. The king of one of the neighbouring kingdoms once decided he would appoint as his chief minister one of these intelligent people.

So he set a test to see who was the wisest. He sent his messenger to court with a strange message, 'I want a person who can bring me fresh vegetables grown in the soil of your kingdom. He should also bring with him a pot full of intelligence.' Now, to get to the neighbouring kingdom, it was a good two months' chariot ride. So even if someone started off with fresh vegetables, they would be rotten by the time he reached there.

Even the wise king was perplexed. One young man from his court, however, knew the solution. He asked the king to give him a cart full of soil, manure and lots of vegetable seeds and saplings. He sowed these in the soil and set off with the cart tied to the rear of his chariot. He also planted a pumpkin plant, and when the vegetable appeared, tied a pot over it, so when the pumpkin grew, it would fill the entire pot.

By the time he reached his destination, he had a good crop of vegetables grown in the soil of his kingdom and freshly plucked. The pumpkin too had grown and now filled the entire pot. He took a big basket of the vegetables and the pumpkin in the pot and appeared before the king.

The king was delighted to see the vegetables but puzzled by the pot. What did it mean? 'I have got intelligence in this pot,' said the young man. 'Now you have to see how you can extract it without breaking the pot.'

The king was pleased. This was a very clever answer to his strange message. But he wanted to test the man some more. So he set before him three wooden dolls, all identical. He said, 'These three are identical, but one is better than the others. Which one would that be?'

The young man asked for a piece of wire. Then he inserted it through the ears of one doll. The wire appeared from the other ear. Next he inserted it through the ears of the second doll. The wire came out of the doll's mouth. But when he inserted the wire from the ear of the third doll, it remained stuck inside. He held up the last doll and said, 'This is the best. In a court, if you told a secret to the first doll it would not understand its importance and take out from one ear what it heard from the other. The second type will hear you, but immediately talk about it to others. The third kind will keep the secret safe in its head.'

The king was even more pleased now. But he wanted to set a final test. 'Here are three rings, with green, red and blue stones respectively. Let us assume they are magical stones. The red ring will give the person wearing it good ideas. The green ring will help the person carry out these ideas in normal circumstances. The blue one will help the person carry out the idea in any circumstance. In a court, who should wear which ring?'

The man thought and said, 'The king should wear the red ring, as he needs to get good ideas. The chief minister should wear the green one, as he needs to carry out these ideas in times of peace. The commander of the army should wear the blue ring, as he needs to carry out the ideas in difficult times.'

The king now knew he had before him a brilliant young man. He was made the chief minister and served the king for many years.

## 36

## A CURE FOR LAZINESS

Basheer had promised himself that he would marry a girl who was as intelligent and hardworking as he was. Once, he went to a country far from his own to do some trade. He stayed in a little inn there. The innkeeper had a daughter called Ayesha. The minute Basheer saw her, he was struck by her beauty, and most of all, her big, bright eyes.

Basheer had to stay in that village for a while and he got to know the villagers quite well. Among them was an old man, perhaps the oldest man in the village. In the evenings, the villagers would gather around him and he would ask them witty questions, to which the youngsters had to give quick answers. One day, as Basheer was walking around in the evening, he heard the old man say, 'I have one sheep. How can I use it to earn some money without killing or selling it?'

There was silence. Then Ayesha spoke up. 'I know, Great Uncle. If I had a sheep, I would look after it very well. When it became fat and healthy, I would sell its wool, milk and dung and make a lot of money. Perhaps I would buy two more sheep and soon have a flock!'

That was a clever answer, thought Basheer, and he stopped to hear a few more questions and answers. Next, the old man asked, 'How would you capture fire in paper and hold the air in your hand?'

Again it was Ayesha who answered, 'I would use a paper lamp and a hand fan.'

The old man had one more question: 'My sister's husband's brother-in-law's wife's friend's son is married to your cousin. What is my sister to me?'

Ayesha said promptly, 'Your sister will remain a sister to you.'

By now Basheer had heard enough. Here was a really intelligent woman—his ideal bride. He met Ayesha's father, who agreed happily to have his daughter marry this sober young man. Soon the two got married and set off for Basheer's village.

When Ayesha reached the village and saw her new house, she realized Basheer was a very rich man. There were servants here to wait on her every wish, cooks to rustle up the most wonderful meals and gardeners to look after Basheer's vast gardens and orchards. There was no need for her to lift a finger! Ayesha decided she liked this new way of living and slowly she lost her earlier hard-working nature. There were enough people who wanted to be friends with her now that she was rich, and soon she gathered a group of good-for-nothing lazy friends around herself. They did nothing but eat and gossip the whole day.

A few years passed, and no one from Ayesha's own village would have been able to recognize her, so fat and lazy was she now. Then one day she fell sick. Doctors came, they examined her, asked all kinds of questions, scratched their heads, and prescribed medicines. But Ayesha still didn't get well.

Finally, word reached her father's village. And the person who was saddest to hear about Ayesha was the very old man who used to throw those riddles at her. He decided he would do something to bring back the clever, sweet Ayesha of old. He reached her house and announced he would stay there for a while. In return, he promised to cure her of her illness. Ayesha and Basheer agreed and the old man started staying with them.

The next day the treatment began. The man said, 'You will get well only if you eat the special food I cook for you. No one must come to the house and it should stay sparkling clean at all hours.' Ayesha agreed. So the man cooked a small meal for her and left it in a box a few yards away from the main house. Ayesha would have to walk up to it. It was a simple meal, but tasty. And Ayesha had to work so hard to keep the house clean without the help of servants that she was always hungry; whatever she ate tasted wonderful.

Many months passed like this. Ayesha got used to the work and the new food habits. She started learning how to help with her husband's business and in the fields. With no one to gossip with, she had to think through everything on her own, and slowly her old intelligence shone forth. Every day she went to bed tired out and slept soundly. The next morning she woke up at the crack of dawn, refreshed, and started her day's work. She realized she was happier now than she had ever been.

She went to the old man and said, 'I am cured at last, Great Uncle. What was the secret of your therapy? I will tell my friends about it too.'

The old man laughed and said, 'I did not do anything. Once upon a time, when you were poor, you were healthy and active. You used to do all the work yourself. Then you became rich and lazy. You had so many maids to do all the work for you. I only gave you healthy food and made you work like before. Your illness disappeared. Rich or poor, it is good to do our own work and be fit. You were always a bright girl, and now you use your energy for better things.'

Basheer was listening to all this silently. Now he smiled. He knew the Ayesha he had loved and married was back for good.

## THE MAGIC DRUM

Ramachandra and Rama were an old couple. They had worked very hard and saved every paisa they possibly could, to make their dream come true. They wanted to visit Kashi and offer puja to Lord Vishwanath. They saved for many years, and one day were delighted to find they had enough money for their pilgrimage.

They set out on the long and dangerous journey. They had been warned that there would be many thieves on the way and hence were quite careful with their belongings, especially their small pouch. They had put all their money in it.

On the way to Kashi they passed Souveera, a small village. They had heard that it was a good place to stay the night. So the old couple decided to stop and spend the night in one of the dormitories there.

Kamesh, the owner of that dormitory, told the couple to leave their belongings with him and freshen up for dinner. But the two refused to do so. Rama sat holding the bag containing their money while Ramachandra went to take a bath. After he finished, he sat holding the bag and Rama went to wash up. Then they had dinner, chatted with Kamesh for some time and went into their room.

They decided to use the pouch as a pillow and Ramachandra slept with it under his head. The first thing they did when they woke up the next morning was check for their money bag. To their horror, they discovered it was missing! While they were sleeping, the lodge-owner Kamesh and his wife had entered the room and removed the bag from under the old man's head.

The two cried in despair; now they would not be able to complete their pilgrimage. Then they went to Kamesh to complain. But Kamesh coolly replied, 'I don't know anything about your bag. You are old, you must have dropped it somewhere. This is an honest person's lodge.'

After some more arguments, the elderly couple walked out clutching their small bag of clothes and some food. As they walked through the village, they told many people their story. A teacher, sitting and teaching his students under a tree, heard them and decided they should be given justice. He told them to go to the city, where Krishnakant, the king's counsellor, lived. He was famous for his sense of fairness.

Krishnakant heard their story and said, 'I have a drum in my house. If you tell the truth in front of the drum, it starts beating by itself. You come to my house tomorrow morning and carry the drum to the court. On your way, tell the drum your story. I will send word to Kamesh to come and carry the drum back in the afternoon. I will see how the drum behaves and be ready with the verdict in the evening.'

The next morning, Rama and Ramachandra started walking with the magic drum to the court. It was very heavy. The court was at a distance and the two were soon tired. They saw a big banyan tree and decided to rest in its shade. They put the drum down and sat under the tree.

Rama said, 'We will never get justice in a strange kingdom. Let us go back home.'

Ramachandra replied, 'I was so careful with the money, yet we lost it. Maybe the lord does not wish us to visit him.'

As soon as he said these words, the sound of beating came from the drum. The old couple was very happy. 'We may have no witness, but god knows we are speaking the truth.' Then they stood up and, after drinking some water from a nearby stream, they picked up the drum. To their surprise, they found it had become much lighter. 'God must have heard us,' they told each other happily. 'That is why he has made our load lighter.'

In the afternoon, it was the turn of Kamesh and his wife to carry the drum back from the court. They too found it very heavy and decided to sit under the big tree to rest. As soon as they sat down, the wife started blaming her husband. 'Why did you have to steal the money? Now see what a mess we are in.'

Kamesh replied angrily, 'You are a good one to blame me. Who unlocked the door and showed me where the pouch was kept? Anyway, do you really believe this is a magical drum? I think it is all a lie.'

Now Krishnakant himself opened the top of the drum and jumped out. 'I am the witness. I have heard every word you said, and also what Rama and Ramachandra said. You will return the stolen money and also pay three times more as penalty.'

Rama and Ramachandra were delighted when they heard the verdict. They went on to complete their pilgrimage in comfort, all the while blessing Krishankant and his magic drum!